THE IM...

THE
PENITENT

PART III

A. KEITH CARREIRO

COPPER
BEECH
PRESS

The Immortality Wars: The Penitent – Part III. Copyright © 2017 A. Keith Carreiro. Produced and printed by Stillwater River Publications. All rights reserved. Written and produced in the United States of America. This book may not be reproduced or sold in any form without the expressed, written permission of the authors and publisher.
Visit our website at **www.StillwaterPress.com** for more information.

First Stillwater River Publications Edition 2019.

Library of Congress Control Number: 2016956319

ISBN-10: 1-950339-12-2
ISBN-13: 978-1-950339-12-9

1 2 3 4 5 6 7 8 9 10
Written by A. Keith Carreiro.
Cover art by Hollis Michaela. www.hollismichaela.com
Published by Stillwater River Publications, Pawtucket, RI, USA.

Publisher's Cataloging-In-Publication Data
(Prepared by The Donohue Group, Inc.)

Names: Carreiro, A. Keith, author.
Title: The Penitent. Part III / A. Keith Carreiro.
Description: First Stillwater River Publications edition. | Pawtucket, RI, USA : Stillwater
    River Publications, 2019. | Series: The immortality wars
Identifiers: ISBN 9781950339129 | ISBN 1950339122
Subjects: LCSH: Soldiers--Fiction. | Good and evil--Fiction. | Priests--Fiction. | Courage-
    Fiction. | Speculative fiction. | GSAFD: Christian fiction. | LCGFT: Allegories. |
    Fantasy fiction.
Classification: LCC PS3603.A774375 P463 2019 | DDC 813/.6--dc23

This is a work of fiction. Except for reference(s) made in regard to the overall Christian concept(s) of belief, any similarity between the characters and situations within its pages and places or persons, living or dead, is unintentional and co–incidental.

The views and opinions expressed in this book are solely those of the author and do not necessarily reflect the views and opinions of the publisher.

Connect with Keith on his website
or other social media platforms:

https://immortalitywars.com
https://www.facebook.com/keith.carreiro.33
https://instagram.com/immortalitywars/
https://twitter.com/immortalitywars
https://www.linkedin.com/in/keith-carreiro-5040aa17/
https://www.goodreads.com/author/show/15959901
https://reedsy.com/author/a-keith-carreiro

To the storytellers in our lives...

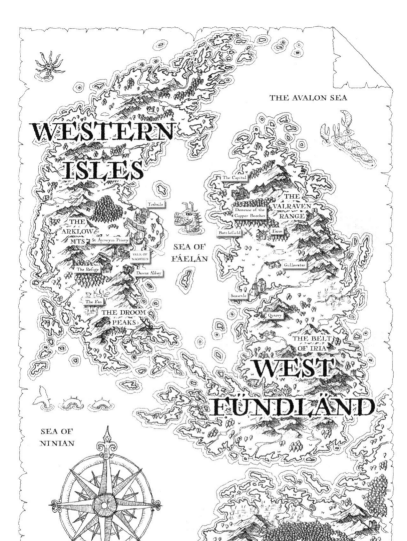

THE AVALON SEA

WESTERN
ISLES

THE
ARKLOW
MTS

St Aynyus Priory

FALS OF
NAOISIUS

The Refuge

Dawns Abbey

The Fen

THE DROOM
PEAKS

SEA OF
FÁELÁN

Trubaile

The Capital

THE
VALRAVEN
RANGE

Demesne of the
Copper Beeches

BattleGield ✕

Exrm

Gullawater

Seascale

Quarry

THE BELT
OF IRIA

WEST
FÜNDLÄND

SEA OF
NINIAN

JB '20

ACKNOWLEDGMENTS

Psalm 51:16-17 is from The Living Bible copyright © 1971. Used by permission of Tyndale House Publishers, Inc., Carol Stream, Illinois 60188. All rights reserved.

Shakespeare, William. "Literature Network – William Shakespeare – King Lear – Act 5. Scene III." *The Literature Network*. Jalic Inc., 2000-2016. Web. 12 Mar. 2016. http://www.online-literature.com /Shake speare/kinglear/27/

Spenser, Edmund. "Edmund Spenser – The Faerie Queene – Canto I." *The Literature Network*. Jalic Inc., 2000-2016. Web. 12 Mar. 2016. http://www.online-literature.com/edmund-spenser/ facrie-queene/2/

A debt of thanks to Dawn and Steven R. Porter, Stillwater River Publications, for their help and expertise in making this print-on-demand novel possible.

Without Hollis Machala's visual expertise, her creative genius, and kind patience with me in helping develop the exterior and interior formatting of *the Penitent*, this story would still be in manuscript form. A deep debt of thanks goes to her for her invaluable assistance in helping make an idea be beautifully visible.

Jamie Forgetta is a freelance illustrator, author, and designer who helped me visualize the settings for *the Penitent*. Her maps of St. Åyrwyus Priory and of Seascale are found, respectively, in the second and third books of the first trilogy of *The Immortality Wars* series. Many thanks to her for her superbly crafted visual work. Her patience is amazing and her ability to collaborate effectively with an author having no visual talent whatsoever is a miracle. The quality of her work speaks for itself. She helped inspire some of the names of streets in the Seascale map and helped in getting some of the mountain ranges named for the main map depicting the setting of *the Penitent*. Her website is https://jamieforgetta. wixsite.com/portfolio

The map of the setting for *the Penitent* was drawn by Jog Brogzin. I first became aware of his artistry on Instagram. After contacting him and asking if he would create a map for me, he kindly agreed to do so. From the first preliminary drawings, all the way to their completion, I was fascinated with his talent and gift for rendering exactly what I was seeking in a map that not only portrays the featured landmarks of the story, but also casts its own spell of imaginative mystery and legend. Jog discovered fantasy cartography back in 1993. He explores worlds with his pen as if he was travelling there in person in his client's world, allowing his imagination to bridge the gap. He makes maps for authors and RPG publishers. His work can be found at the following link: https://www.facebook.com/jogbrogzin

Thanks, also, to my daughter, Chelsea Snyder, for her help in designing the cover, especially at the beginning stages of design.

A deep and abiding thanks goes to Carolyn for her support of this story, and for her helping edit the first draft. The same thanks goes to Kellie Kilgore for her editing help as well.

I have seen the day, with my good biting falchion
I would have made them skip…

— William Shakespeare (1564–1616),
King Lear (1608)
— Act V, Scene iii, ll. 276 & 277

Led with delight, they thus beguile the way,
Vntill the blustering storme is ouerblowne;
When weening to returne, whence they did stray,
They cannot finde that path, which first was showne,
But wander too and fro in ways vnknowne,
Furthest from end then, when they nearest weene,
That makes them doubt, their wits be not their owne:
So many paths, so many turnings seene,
That which of them to take, in diuerse doubt they been.

— Edmund Spenser (1552–1599), *The Faerie Qveene* (1590)
— The First Book of The Faerie Qveene *Contayning*
— The Legende of the Knight of the Red Crosse, *or* of Holinesse
—Canto I, Stanza X

[16] You don't want penance;[a] if you did, how gladly I would do it!
You aren't interested in offerings burned before you on the altar.
[17] It is a broken spirit you want—remorse and penitence. A broken
and contrite heart, O God, you will not ignore.

— Psalm 51:16 & 17 (*The Living Bible*)

Footnotes:
[a]Psalm 51:16 *penance*, literally "a sacrifice"

PROLOGUE | PROPOSITIONS SIX*

The singularity that is inevitably coming will be man and Lucifer's chance to carve out a place; if not yet above, but alongside, the Creator's. Mankind will truly learn what it means to <u>dis</u>assemble. The rest of us will be brought into this <u>dys</u>topic[40] montage[41] of evil playing itself out presently on the world canvas in a vast sense of dis*ease. It will be a contagion of mind and a pandemic of conscience fluorescing into all levels of humanity's values at greater and exponentially increasing rates. There will be an avalanche of deceit in which people will earnestly embrace as the truth.*

An intelligent person considers possibilities; an educated one objectively examines ideas and entertains those that are opposite of his or her own predilections.[42] Nevertheless, this scenario that engages us so fiercely now, is one in which a wise person prepares for the worst while hoping for the best. This wise individual selects a strategy, picks a perspective, and makes a conceptual choice dance into practice, especially in order to save the lives of the people s/he loves.*

If we but listen figuratively to such wisdom, we could at least consider my statement here as a thought experiment—an ideational exercise. Affectively, I am sure that it translates well into a trenchant cry in at least three of the world's three great Abrahamic religions: "Gird your loins with the full armor of God.[246] The angels will trumpet[247] in Armageddon.[248] The seals will be opened.[249] The vials will be poured out[250]: The Four Horsemen[251] will canter forth an Apocalypse[252] unto the world's attention."

These occurrences are ancient in their determination to happen. They are inexorable in their proleptic[156] demand for such reality to blossom into our own time, and their very need to unfold into a preordained, historical manifestation only indicates impatient hesitation on their behalf, as well as the momentum guiding them; yet, they will but presently ensue in full force.

Such causes await their attendant effects; they have to proceed because all the forces and omens[51] are assembling into play for them to ignite into being, into an outpouring that includes mythology, legend and *wisdom equally being awakened. Thus, today I await for the Cumaean sibyl[016] to offer her insight into the future; I anticipate a fifteenth book of the Sibylline Oracles[017] to be newly found and read to mankind; and, I pray that I live to hear the voices of a Daniel and a Matthew, a thaumaturge, a nabi or a Tay al-Ard speak aloud of it to me.*

I envy Simeon who in his old *age still tarried on Earth, within the holy temple of ancient Jerusalem, waiting for the consolation of Israel.[14-15]*

-Professor Melvin Tobin, Ph.D.
-Cambridge, Massachusetts, Old Earth

Statement first excerpted from a retirement speech, "U†opia Imperiled," given by Dr. Tobin at the Harvard Club.

Tobin, M. (2156, July 15). †The philosophical primacy[1] of intelligence engineering[2] permeating throughout advanced evolutionary intervention.**56** The Journal of Ideation & Consilience, **H**ologram **C**odex 18: 2287.299 | 12 – **NASCENT:** 2057-2058. Retrieved Epicycle 07, 2252

CHAPTER ONE

He tried not to remember what had just happened. He just did not want to see the images of ruin around him. The young man had learned, so it felt to him, that the matters of the day always intruded their tyranny over him. There was just no permanent escape from suffering. *It is always around*, he thought.

He let the walls of isolation down from around him. Myra was weeping uncontrollably. He smelled the all–pervading rot of Ünger's corpse filling his senses. A crimson, purple light radiated from the Sentinel Tree. Tom was on his knees holding Myra tightly in his arms. He had a stunned, haunted look on his face. Tears fell from his eyes. The place where Alicia had been standing with Mary in her arms was literally seared away from the ground around it.

The young man became upset, then angry, over the shock, evil and injustice over what had just happened. He worked himself up into a furor.

Pall stood up. He walked over to where the largest remaining piece left of the monster was still standing. Pieces of the creature were still falling away from it. On the ground was a medium–sized branch. He looked at his boots with the thought of kicking the dead body over onto the ground. Pall decided he was not as disgusted with the situation as he could have been. Anger fully returned to him and it was replete with fury. He picked up the bough and rammed it into the center of violence that had been Ünger.

He pushed the body just inside the drip line, right underneath the outermost leaves of the tree. Pall then went over to the wagon. He picked up a shovel and a pitchfork. With these two tools, he gathered together as much of the demon's body as he could find.

While occupied in this task, he heard a sound that his father's forge might have made when it was heating up to the desired temperature for working iron and steel. He looked over at where he had deposited the main trunk of the beast's body. Light from the crown and roots of the tree converged on it. What was left of the Ünger vibrated, became insubstantial and then just disappeared from view. The branch that had been thrust into its carcass thumped unharmed to the ground.

Occupied solely in this task of cleaning up the foulness around him, he gradually became aware that his shirttail was being tugged. He looked down to where something or someone was yanking at his clothing. Myra was on his left side, away from where he was holding a pitch fork full of Ünger.

"Can I help you, Pilgrim?" she asked.

He looked at her forlorn shape and turned to look at her father. Tom was on his feet, trying to take in the catastrophe around him.

Tears fell finally from Pall's eyes.

"Yes," he answered her directly and simply.

He got down on his knees and looked at her. She ran into his arms and tried to console him of her mother's loss.

"Myra," he said, "you are a very brave girl. I am going to bring pieces of this thing the tree killed over to where the big one just disappeared."

"I know. I saw the tree make it go away," she offered to explain.

He nodded his head to her. "Good, don't touch them, but make sure the pieces I place around the tree are in that same spot but in a circle around the Sentinel."

"I understand, Pall," the little girl said solemnly.

Before he started his grisly task of gathering together Ünger's remains, he said to her, "Let me know how I'm doing."

Pall heard Tom walk to the wagon and retrieve some tools. He looked over and as the light from the tree illuminated everything around it in sharp relief, he could see that Tom had picked up a shovel, saw and sledge hammer. He was carrying them, along with the branch Pall used to move the monster, out into the field where the copper beech tree could be seen in its entirety.

Pall went back to his task of cleaning up the remaining pieces of Ünger. Finishing his grim work, Pall went to Myra and walked her over to where her father was completing what he was doing in the field.

Tom watched them approach him. When they were almost at his side he explained, "Nothin's left me and Myra from them," he pointed to the two shallow graves he had dug.

"So the least I can do is honor their memory here near this sacred tree that saved you, Myra and me from that wretched wreck of horror."

He crossed the tool head ends of the sledge hammer and shovel together to make a rough cradle for the bough he had brought over with him. He cut the branch in two and sharpened their ends into a point with the axe. He then cut a diagonal notch at the other end of each one. Taking the two pieces of wood one at a time, the cooper used the sledge hammer to pound the sharp ends into the ground at the head of each grave. When they were set the way he wanted them, Tom reached into his pants pocket and removed a large, and a small, piece of leather from it.

The cooper knelt down before the mock graves and inset the large one onto the pole to his left. He said, "She would put this one in her hair and the smaller one in Mary's. It's the only thing I can think of to do...."

4

Tears welled up in his eyes and spilled freely down his face.

He did the same with the smaller piece of leather to his right.

Tom stood up.

Both men started to walk away back to the tree.

Myra exclaimed, "Wait, we need to say a prayer!"

Tom hung his head lower than it was, then quickly stood up straighter. "You're right, little one. I'm sorry."

"It's okay, Da," she said to him consolingly.

"Pall," Tom said, "will you say somethin?"

Pall took a deep breath and sighed, "Yes, gladly; it will be an honor."

Looking down at the graves Tom had dug and finished over, as well as the two stakes upright in the meadow's soil adorned with the two, simple leather hairbands, Pall said as a eulogy,

"I did not know either Alicia or Mary long. But the time I spent with them is a gift of eternity. We became family together. And, as a result, these moments became precious to me. I know that you, Lord, look upon them as being beyond value. As members of your family, I ask that you take them into your dwelling place and soothe their tears and let them rest in the peace of your arms. Pray provide us, the ones left behind in this place of strife and death, the grace to go on to honor their memory in the good we can do for others."

"Thank you, Pall," Tom said softly.

Myra gave Pall a hug and a pat on one of his shoulders.

The three of them walked back to the wagon. They stood under the tree with their hands held together, looking at it with wonder.

In a steady, small voice, Myra said to the copper beech, "Thank you, Sentinel, for saving us. Please take good care of my Ma, Alicia, and my sister Mary."

The tree cast its light steadily around them.

"I'm for hitchin up the horses and getting back on the road," Tom said. "I don't think I can stay here much longer. If I don't go now, I may never be able to leave here."

"Okay, Tom," responded Pall. "Give me a rope when we're all set to go. Tie it to me and the front hitch to the team and I'll go on ahead on the road in front of the horses to make sure it's good for them to go over."

"Take one of the lanterns. I'll light it now from the fire we still got goin. You can use it to help you see where you'll be walkin," Tom advised.

"The tree's light and then the partial light from the moon will help us guide our way, too," Pall offered as reasons to get back on the road to Gullswater.

There was not much to pack up in the wagon. Most of it was already in place. They secured the fire, putting it out thoroughly. The team was hitched. Tom put Myra on the wagon. He took the reins in his hands, and with Pall's help, they led the horses and wagon back onto the road.

Just before Pall was in place to lead the team down the road, he looked back at the tree glowing in all its glory in the field.

"Thank you," he said to it.

CHAPTER TWO

Pall had been leading the horses, Tom and Alicia, on the Gullswater Road for almost three hours without any undue incident occurring. The dirt road was well built. There was a crude camber to it that spread the water to either side, and despite the recent rains, the surface, for the most part, was smooth and uniform. There were areas, particularly where the roadbed consisted of softer packed down soil, in which grooves were deeply scored from the constant traffic of other wagons passing over it. As there were no other travelers on the road this late at night, Tom had no problem letting the wagon slide into them and following the marks until they ended.

Myra was sleeping on the small mattress in the wagon bed that both twins had used since the start of their journey toward a new life. Almost the moment after Tom and Pall started on the road in earnest toward Gullswater, she fell asleep against her father's side. They had stopped momentarily so that Tom could put his only remaining daughter in a more comfortable position to rest.

She's all that I have left.

Thoughts of his family, at first, raced through his mind. He felt as though he was going to fall into a deep pit of sorrow he would never be able to climb out of again.

Think about somethin else.

Mercifully, his memories stopped bedeviling him. He heard the creaking of the wagon as it moved over the darkened road. The sideboards gave a grunted rattle as the wheels went over the uneven surface. The traces, tugs and harness lines connecting the horses to it creaked in an intermittent pattern that accompanied the sound of their hooves. He smelled the night air and sighed a deep breath.

One of the horses snorted.

Tom began nodding off. To prevent himself from dozing, he asked Pall to talk with him about anything, just so it would help him stay awake and alert.

"Forgive me for asking you, then," Pall said. "What will you do now, Tom, especially after what just...." He could not finish his question and decided to ask, instead, "I'm sorry, I don't mean to be so rude, but will you still take the cooper's job in Gullswater?"

Tom knew how difficult it was for Pall to ask him such a delicate question. Yet, he was glad for it to be asked of him; it helped him focus his attention on an answer he just did not have set in his mind at the moment.

"I don't know, Pall, it's the first time I've put any thought to it. I think I'm in shock. And, I know for sure, Myra is too."

"I think you need more time to sort everything out," the young soldier suggested.

"Yes, I do. How long does it take, do you think, for folks like Myra and me to get a hold of what we're supposed to do?"

"I guess..." Pall thought out loud and paused to end his statement. He stopped walking and lifted the lantern high and then low to get a varied perspective on the road just ahead of him. Seeing nothing that caused him any concern or alarm, he started walking again.

"I guess everyone's different in how they take such an awful loss when they experience it," he said.

As Tom thought about what next to say, he remained alert to the noises the wagon was making and how it was moving over the road's surface. He paid heed again to the jiggling and shifting of the leather reins, to the harnesses and to the tack on the horses. The cooper was attentive to the mood of Tom and Alicia as they steadfastly pulled the big wagon after Pall's lead ahead of them.

"I think Myra and me'll take the cooper's job in Gullswater for now," Tom speculated. "I won't be breakin a promise after tellin the town fathers I would take the job. It would be wrong of me not to take it. Alicia would want me to work there. It'll force me to do somethin other than just thinkin about what happened. Maybe that's the best way goin about dealin with it until I have a firmer grasp on what we're doin."

10

"Sounds good, Tom," Pall said reassuringly to his friend.

They were quiet for a while. They traveled slowly, but steadily and safely, for another half mile.

Tom asked Pall, "What will you do when we reach the town?"

"Like you and Myra, my friend, I don't know. Maybe I will just stay a bit, as well, to get my legs back under me. I'm trying to sort out who I am and where to go. I was hoping to meet a friend of mine, but I'm not sure he's been, or going to be, in Gullswater. I guess I'll see what happens once I'm there."

"If I can be of any help, Pall, just let me know. You're welcome to stay with Myra and me for the time."

"Thanks, Tom. I won't be staying long. I just pray that I will figure out what to do that's right for me."

They were quiet again. They went about another mile.

Tom, not realizing he had fallen asleep, jerked awake. He tried focusing on what he could hear was happening around him, but he could not chase away the deep torpor flooding his senses.

"Pall, I am quite spent and I think we need to call a halt. Let's find a decent place to stop off the side of the road and rest until daylight comes round again."

"Okay," Pall responded. "Sounds like a very good idea. I've gone through at least six candles. Let's stop the team and I'll go up and back down the road to see if there is a place where we can put up the wagon."

Pall brought the lead rope he was using back to Tom. He put a fresh candle in the night lantern and proceeded to go up ahead of the team on the left side of the roadway.

Tom watched the lantern's light almost fade away completely. He saw the light placed down onto the road. It remained in the same place for a few heartbeats. He saw that Pall had picked up the lantern again and crossed to the opposite side of the road, which was to Tom's right.

The lantern grew brighter as it started approaching the wagon. About two hundred or so feet away, Pall halted and then brought the light off to the side of the road. It was not long after he stopped that he came quickly back to the wagon.

Upon drawing even with the team of horses, Pall held Alicia's bridle. He patted her on her nose and talked softly to her. When he was done comforting her, he informed Tom, "Just ahead, there's an excellent place off the right side of the road for us to pull over and stay until we're better rested."

"Thanks, Pall; let's stop there for now. I don't want to press our luck anymore movin the team in the dark of the night."

Pall clicked his teeth together and urged the horses on to the place he had found for them to rest from their labor of hauling the wagon. It was as if they sensed that the humans had made up their minds to stop the foolishness of being on the road at night. They snorted and shook themselves in eagerness to get there.

Soon enough, Tom and Pall pulled off the road and found more than ample space to stop the wagon and to settle down for the remainder of the evening. They took care of the horses, made sure the brake was set on the wagon and began the process of getting ready for sleep.

Tom went in the back of the wagon and made his bed next to his daughter.

Pall pulled his mattress out of the wagon and put it on a canvas that he had placed on the ground underneath the wagon bed. He literally fell down upon it from exhaustion.

Weary and spent from the torment of battle, the loss of loved ones, and in a state of denial about the terrible pain and loneliness brought down upon them, the three travelers soon fell asleep into the quiet remains of the night.

CHAPTER THREE

Morning light failed to break their slumber. It was the creaking of a wagon passing by them on the road, and the whinnying of Alicia and Tom to the team leading it, that woke Myra. She, in turn, woke her father. Father and daughter proceeded to get up from their rest and, in moving around in the wagon above him, Pall awoke as well.

They had plain and simple fare for breaking their fast. No fire was started and cooked over. They stayed in their same clothes.

Before Tom had anything to eat, he checked on his horses. He brushed them down after he fed them.

No one said much until Myra, who was watching Pall eat his breakfast, addressed him politely, "Thanks, Pilgrim, for helping lead Da and me away in the dark from the tree of light."

"You're welcome, Myra," he responded.

"Weren't you scared being out in front of the wagon in the dark?" she asked him.

"No, I felt very safe," he assured her.

"Why did you feel safe?" she queried him again.

"Because you were in the wagon protecting us," he said with a straight face to her.

She looked closely at Pall to see if he was joking with her. When she could not tell if he was being serious or not, she giggled. "That's just silly; a three–year–old little girl makes you feel safe."

He nodded his head at her. "Yes, I felt safe because there was a three–year–old little girl named Myra in the wagon whose love for her family is greater than anything I know in the whole wide world."

Myra tried puzzling out what Pall had just told her. She brightened at a thought she was entertaining and said, "Love can help people walk in the dark; right, Pall?"

"Yes, Myra, I could not have said it any better than you just did, little one," he said admiringly to her.

She kept her gaze on him as her eyes welled with tears. "Do you think the love me and Da have for Ma and Mary will help them walk in the dark, too?"

Pall glanced over at Tom who was listening closely to the conversation they were having with one another. "I think that, if they were in the dark, they found their way because you and your Da's love helped them get home. I don't believe they're in the dark any longer."

Myra smiled at the young man. She leaned her head against her father's shoulder who was sitting by her side on the driver's bench of the wagon.

Pall had stood next to the wagon while eating his food. He had put the horses in their traces and they were ready to get back on the road to Gullswater.

"Thanks, Pall," Tom said, "that was a kindness you gave Myra and me, as well–framed as the fight you gave the beast last night. I will never forget what you did to help save us."

"You're welcome, Tom. I just wish I could have done more. Truly it was the Sentinel Tree that saved us all."

"Nevertheless," Tom insisted, "thank you."

Pall smiled back at the cooper, but it was a difficult one to show his friend, especially when he was still very close to tears. "I think I'll walk a bit beside the wagon once we get going."

They spent the rest of the day traveling towards Gullswater. It was late afternoon when they arrived there. They saw people going about their business. They seemed unconcerned about the strangers in their midst.

Pall was beginning to think that everyone in the town was just rude. Yet, to his pleasant surprise, when Tom asked for directions to the livery, they were very polite and cordial to the young workman. Everyone he asked gave him the information willingly and cheerfully.

Soon, Tom drove his team of horses to the front of the livery stable.

16

The livery was doing a brisk business. It was awhile before the proprietor came out of the stable to talk with them. When he found out that Tom was the cooper the town had sent for, he became even more personable than before on first greeting them.

"Well," he said to Tom. "Welcome to Gullswater! My name's Lucas. I'll have my apprentice show you to the cooper's workshop. I think you'll like it. A portion of it's on the river, which is excellent for buyin and sellin what you make. Lots of room for a family like yours…."

Lucas stopped because he did not see any presence of a wife, or a mother, to Myra in the wagon. Seeing the expressions of loss on their faces, he politely and quickly changed the topic. "Take a look around. The town's major merchant and craft guilds got together and pretty much set everything up. The place should be ready to go."

Lucas paused a bit, and then added, "Go on over, take a look around and let me know what you think of it, Tom."

"Thanks, Mr. Lucas," Tom said.

"Think nothin of it. Take your time over there. Get comfortable first. I'll come and see you round noontime tomorrow. Got to get goin now. We're fairly busy today. If I'm not round to spoil my customers, they get upset."

17

He waved goodbye to them and walked back into the gloom of the stable's wide flung sliding doors.

Just as he disappeared inside, a young boy came out and walked over to the driver's seat of the wagon where Tom awaited him. "I'm Lucas Junior," he informed them, "but you can just call me Junior, that'll be good enough for me."

"Hello, Junior. I'm Tom. This here assistant to my right is Myra, and that's Pall–with a double L– yonder on the other side of the wagon."

"Hi, Junior!" Myra exclaimed. "You going to show us to our new home?"

"Yes," he said beaming up at Myra who was sitting next to Tom.

"Hop aboard, Junior," Tom invited.

Without being asked twice, Junior jumped with great agility onto the wagon and soon was giving Tom directions to the cooper's workshop.

When they arrived at their long awaited destination, Junior jumped off the wagon. "Gotta get back to the stable. The old man'll miss me and then there'll be trouble in it for me too," he said to them just before he sprinted away back to see Lucas.

All three of them stayed on the wagon for a while. They stared at the workshop in front of them.

Tom looked at it with an appraising eye. He liked what he saw. With a deep sigh, he said, "May as well get the hoop placed on the cask and go look at our new home."

He stepped down from the wagon and helped Myra get off as well. After staring some more at the place, he started walking to the front door. He stopped and looked back at the wagon. Seeing Pall next to it, he said to him, "C'mon now. You're not gettin out of this. Please walk with Myra and me and see where we have a place to live for now."

Pall waved his hand at Tom, indicating that he heard and that he was complying with Tom's request to accompany him into the building. He joined them, and when they got to the front door, Tom opened it. Both men took one of Myra's hands and they lifted her through the door inside the front of the shop. Tom went in next with Pall following close behind him.

They spent the next hour looking around. Tom had to stop his assessment of the place to take care of the horses. They were still patiently waiting outside the front of the shop for someone to take care of them. After Tom and Pall unhitched the team, they brought them into a small stable next to the shop. The two men fed the horses and rubbed them down, praising them aloud for the incredible work they had done in bringing them to Gullswater.

Afterwards, they spent the remainder of the time getting most of the equipment and supplies off the wagon and into the cooper's work space.

They had a supper that was brought over to them by Mrs. Lucas and one of her older daughters. The women did not stay long. They hardly even introduced themselves before they were gone. The food was delicious and plentiful, and they heartily filled their hunger.

They became quiet again, thinking about what could have been and what Alicia might have said about the place, and how the two twins would have been running all over investigating every novel detail of their new home.

Pall shook off the torpor and gloom building around him. "Tom, I'm going to get the mattress you've let me use and bring it in here. I think I'll get to rest early. I'm a lot more tired than I thought I was when I sat down to eat."

Tom nodded at Pall. "I think we'll do the same. We're gonna go upstairs to the loft and sleep there. See you in the mornin, Pall. Thanks for all your help. I couldn't have done it so gracefully without you."

"You're welcome, Tom. Good night."

Father and daughter left the room. Before leaving with Tom, Myra walked over to Pall and gave him a hug. "Good night, Pilgrim," she said. "I love you."

After the little girl expressed her love to him, and they left the room, tears came. He did not remember falling asleep. There was aching grief, then a void for about eight hours while he slept in the dark. No one was there to help him see if the road on which he was travelling was safe.

CHAPTER FOUR

All three of them woke early the next morning because there was a knock at the front door. As Pall had slept in the front room over night, he answered the door. When he opened it, he discovered that Junior was there with food to break their fast.

"That's really very thoughtful of Master and Mrs. Lucas to put together this food for Tom and Myra," Pall told the boy. "And thank you for bringing it over, too," he added.

Junior's face flushed. He gave a big grin at Pall and said, "Aw, it was easy to do. I just brought it over to them."

"True," Pall responded, "but it's the little things like what you just did for Tom and Myra that make the day seem to pass by easier."

Not knowing exactly what to say to Pall's comment, Junior bid goodbye and ran back over to the stables.

Pall closed the door and carried the food Junior had brought over to the Coopers to one of the smaller tables in the room. Just as he set it down on the table, Tom and Myra entered the room.

They exchanged greetings with one another. Pall told Tom about the Lucases sending Junior over to the workshop with the food.

"I'll be goin over there soon," Tom informed Pall, "to let Lucas know that this place is just fine for my purposes. I'll have to ask Mrs. Lucas about someone to help me take care of Myra when I'm workin. What about you, Pall? What are you going to do now that you're in Gullswater?"

Pall looked at Tom and then studied his warrior's hands. He held them up in front of his chest. "They don't look like much, but all they've known is working at my father's forge and fighting."

"You're more than welcome to stay with us; you know that, right?" asked Tom.

"Yes, Tom, it's kind and considerate of you to say so," he said.

"If you need work, I can certainly use your help here," as Tom gave this invitation to Pall, the cooper moved his hand over to his daughter's and held it tenderly.

The young soldier watched them for a moment and said, "I might need to stay here, no more than several days, I think. I need to find a friend of mine and I don't know if that is even possible to do. This morning, I thought I'd go into the town and ask around."

Tom nodded approval at Pall's words. "You know, Pall, what about asking Master Lucas how to go about finding your friend? Lucas sees a lot of people during the day and night and he knows even more of them in the town and surrounding area."

Pall stood up from the table. "Good idea, Tom. Think I will follow your advice. I guess I'll see you later on in the day. Good luck and God bless you this morning."

Pall went over and shook the cooper's hand. Myra gave him a hug, but he could see she was distracted and anxious to get on with exploring her new home more. He thought, *It's good that she has her mind set on wanting to learn more about her new place.*

He walked to the front door. Before he let himself outside, he turned around to them and waved goodbye. They waved back and got up from the table to start their day.

Pall decided he would take Tom's advice and headed over to Lucas' stable. He took the time to absorb his new surroundings. There wasn't much to see, but he knew what he was not seeing and observing could make a huge difference in his success of finding the bowman.

Most people nodded a faint hello to him. He passed a variety of merchants' and craftsmen's shops. There were more people—women, men and children—out on the town roads with him than he had suspected would be there this early in the day.

Arriving at the livery, he was surprised to see Lucas standing in front of the main doors to his stable.

"Had an early rush of customers, n now there's a lull. That'll go by soon enough. What can I do for you this mornin? Pall, isn't it?"

"Yes sir," Pall acknowledged. "Tom suggested I come over and see you about a friend of mine I have been looking for. He said you might be able to get me started."

"Okay, son, describe im to me. What's e do?"

Pall gave Savage's description, but did not tell him all the details of their association with one another.

"I'll ask around and make some inquiries," Lucas answered.

Pall thought the liveryman had avoided answering him directly.

Lucas, seeing Pall getting edgier in his presence, said, "Seems to me a big feller like that would be noticed by folks around here. Let you know later on in the afternoon what I find."

If anyone would have seen or heard of Savage being here, Pall thought, *it would be Lucas.*

"In the meantime, I'd check the Gullswater Tavern," Lucas had kept talking. "Most people stop there when they come to town."

"Thank you, Master Lucas," Pall said on the verge of sounding blatantly suspicious.

He asked the liveryman for the directions to the tavern. They were simple enough. Gullswater was not a very big place.

Lucas went back into the stables with an audible sigh of relief that he let out of his lungs when he was well inside the building.

The young warrior started walking towards the tavern, but he changed his mind and decided to walk around the town and get familiar with what was around him. He did not want to talk with anyone about his search for Savage just yet, either. *Perhaps if I find out more about what's here, I'll get an idea what to do next*, he said to himself.

Pall spent the next several hours walking around the town, going into the shops and examining what was for sale. He watched people interacting with one another, listened as unobtrusively as he could to their conversations, and watched where they went and, if he could do so, what they did when they got there.

At one point in his observations, he found himself along the riverfront. He noticed that almost all of the buildings had a pier or dock on the water from which they could conduct their separate tenants' or owners' businesses by sending and receiving information and goods in either direction on the river. Most of the properties were in good condition.

Oddly enough, there was a collection of seven buildings next to one another that were in poor to rough order. He did not expect to find them in such a neglected state in the middle of the town's waterfront area. They were unkempt, even falling apart. He also observed that, whereas the well–ordered and well–kept buildings had foot traffic going in and out of them, these seven buildings that looked as though they should have already fallen down, had no one visible outside, or inside, them.

He only walked by them once, on the far side of the lane away from the frontage these buildings had onto the road. He did not want to attract any more attention than he had already. His instinct told him that he had been seen and observed from at least two of the buildings.

Noon came and went. Pall went out of the town limits, which was not far at all, and found a quiet, unoccupied spot on the river. He sat down next to it and became mesmerized by the swift flow of its current. He thought of the memories that had been returning to him from his former life. It all still seemed so disconnected. Yet, he did see that his life had been extraordinary for one so young—even miraculous. He thought of his parents, his life as a soldier and the battle from which he had seemingly awoken and that started the journey to his being here, appropriately, on the Forgotten River.

"Maybe if I find transportation on this river," he stated aloud, "and I stay on it long enough, I'll either remember more, or lose what I have now, concerning my identity."

He wanted to find Savage, but he wanted also to find the elite troops of which he had been such an integral part for at least most of the time since he had left his father's forge. He recalled that Savage was with him when the Valravn attacked Pall and uttered the strange prophecy at him. At times, his arm still seemed to burn and itch from the strange bird's blood that fell upon it.

Most of all, though, and back in the deepest part of his mind was the vision of a stunning looking young woman with hazel green eyes, freckles and long red hair. Something happened to him when their eyes met. He could not explain the power of that connection. It seemed to offer a combination of promise and of peril that he did not want to think about; yet, at the same time, he wanted to explore.

The soldiers were calling her "Evangel," *there must be some people around here who know about her.*

He also thought about the moments when he was deeply in touch with God and the miracles that happened to him when the Lord touched him, or when he touched the Lord. The memory of the battle with his young companions against the elite Aeonian veterans was a memory that had just recently resurfaced in his mind.

Praying for the life of Captain Martains alone was exhilarating, even a joyful and humbling act of mercy. Seeing him revive and all those who remained alive do so as well—despite the severity of their wounds—still perplexed and awed him.

He could not deny that they happened. In addition, his contact with the Herald, and the death ship, his connection to the sword and its connection with him, and his contact and battle with Ünger, all made him see that something was pulling at him very powerfully. But these forces tugging for his attention were completely foreign to him. He could not clearly understand their relevance and meaning.

At one moment, he felt poised on the edge of a huge realization of what everything in his life amounted to. At the very next moment, he thought he was about to be lost in a quagmire of confusion and darkness. The deaths of Alicia and her daughter Mary were taking a very heavy toll. He had faced death, as well as sent many opponents into death's arms, but he could not come to grips with these two. He replayed in his mind the fight against Ünger underneath the Sentinel Tree. The coruscations of power that came out of the demon, the seemingly protective power emanating from the tree that eventually took the beast's life away, and the power pouring out of him and the sword, overwhelmed his logic.

Either it's something that doesn't make sense, or is irrational, or it's a level of rational action that I have never considered before now.

Pall shook his head in consternation. There were just too many things to consider.

He looked up at where the sun stood in the sky. He saw that, from its angle where he was observing it, early afternoon was well upon him. He got up on his feet and walked away from the river. He bent his steps toward the tavern, thinking that people must be working up an appetite and a thirst now that could best be quenched and appeased at the Gullswater Tavern at this time of day.

Entering the village once more, he reflected to himself, *I need to find John Savage. He has the answers to many of my questions.*

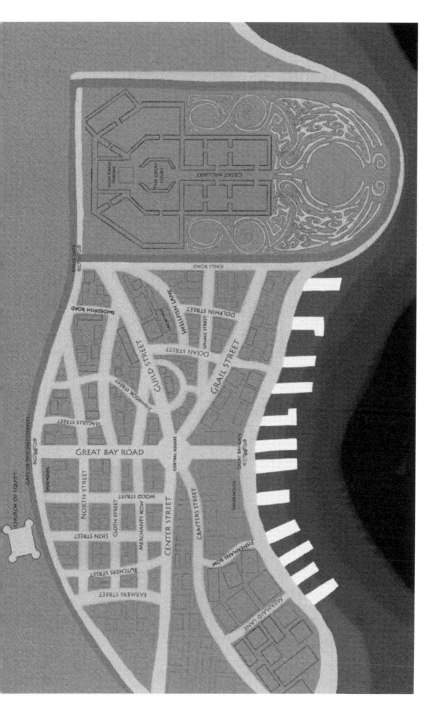

CHAPTER FIVE

Seascale was a major port city in West Fündländ. It was the summer seat of King Ranulf Ealhhere's court. The port was famous for its vast protected harbor and for its temperate summer climate. It was the base for the King's northwestern fleet and it was a major center for maritime commerce. Seascale was the home of sailors and admirals alike. It was a mecca for traders, merchants, and other businessmen in the retail trades. Likewise, the King's army was also headquartered nearby. Soldiers and generals rubbed shoulders with the rest of the populace on the streets, especially when encamped outside the city.

Many wealthy and powerful families also had summer estates, manors and retirement villas within, and in close proximity of, the city. As the King resided in Seascale for half the year, many government officials also lived there, as well. It was cosmopolitan and coarse, sophisticated and seedy. Savage hated it, and thoroughly enjoyed it at the same time. There was never a place to find solitude or peace. But there always was a large number of diverse people residing and visiting the port city. All different walks of life and diverse races of people constituted its population.

Someone like him, who physically stood above the heads and shoulders of almost all the people there, was virtually absorbed into its scene. He became part of the crowd. Everywhere else outside of this summer capital, he became apart from the crowd, not of it. Here he was average.

Away from here he was atypical. It was a very unsettling place to be. Delightful and disconcerting as it was for him, he kept such feelings about the place to himself. He was a quiet, solitary man. He had to be. He was one of the King's most trusted men and one of his best intelligence **gatherers**.

The bowman was quite overdue in meeting with King Ealhhere's Minister of Affairs. Braucus Peredurus had been in this powerful royal post for as long as Savage could remember. The Minister was in charge of all governmental concerns, foreign and domestic. A former commanding general of the previous king's armies, he brought a wealth of experience in political strategy and knowledge about the conduct of war and peace to the Crown. Because of the profound depth of gamesmanship and guts Peredurus brought to the post of Minister of Affairs, he became a very dangerous man, as well as one whose favor was curried by many wanting, and/or having, to deal with power on a national scale.

The Minister's father, Lycidyuse Peredurus, had been head of the admiralty of King Warin Ealhhere's maritime and naval forces. Father and son were very close. Braucus was Lycidyuse's right hand man. The son, at the age of nine, started an apprenticeship of study with his father that lasted until his father's death, when Braucus was thirty–one. The father had urged, inspired and pushed his son into being a soldier, despite the father's tradition of all things being naval.

"In ten years," he first told Braucus when his son began his training with him, "you will be in the officer corps of one of the King's armies. If not a general, you will still command hundreds, if not thousands, of men. Your knowledge of land warfare, combined with mine on the seas, will create a working knowledge and legacy for the future kings of West Fündländ and the Ministry of Affairs. What we will be able to accomplish will be looked upon as a halcyon time of political mastery. It will be called the golden age of our preeminence amongst all the realms of this part of the world."

Savage never made direct contact with the Minister. There were several places in the port city where initial notice to meet with him was made via individuals who stood as proxies for the head of affairs of state. None of them were conventional people. The archer decided he would visit Stephan Sayer's place. Sayer was head of the Great Bay Merchants Guild. He was also one of the chief proprietors of the Great Bay Tavern. Savage knew that chances of getting to Sayer were always good if one went to the tavern instead of the guildhall.

Sayer was part of the ever growing espionage and intelligence network the King and his Minister of Affairs had established, maintained and developed further. The assets, wealth and resources of the royal treasury, its martial and merchant forces and the bureaucratic networks established through the oversight of Lycidyuse and Braucus Peredurus, were some of the finest and most respected throughout the Realm's sphere of influence.

As the King grew ever more powerful and the realm he ruled did likewise, the demand for active and reliable reconnaissance not only grew larger, the appetite for it became insatiable, too. Royalty appreciated and awarded those able to obtain information that gave aid to the Crown in gauging the clout and power of its allies and opponents. The capacity to learn the disposition of his enemies' defenses and forces was not taken lightly.

Seascale was an ideal and natural place for espionage networks to exist. Translators, cryptographers, couriers and royal messengers were used throughout the various and diverse channels set up to do so by the Ministry of Affairs. Peredurus used the guild system as one of his invisible webs of intrigue.

Savage walked to the tavern as though it was something unplanned. He doubled back on his route several times, checking—without appearing to do so—whether or not he was being followed or observed formally. He stopped at a variety of shops in the city, sampled a variety of wares, bargained for some unsuccessfully and purchased his noon meal at several different victualers' stands. To the casual eye, he walked nonchalantly and without a definitive direction or goal in mind.

The bowman first passed by the Great Bay Tavern without seeming to notice that he had done so. His eye was on a vendor selling chestnuts from his cart further up the lane. He bought a small bag from him and retraced his steps. When the archer got even with the tavern, he looked up at the sign above its main door. It was creaking slightly from a wind that was coming off the bay. Savage made a show of deliberating whether or not to go inside.

Shrugging his shoulders as if to say, "I haven't anything better to do," he casually entered the tavern's door.

Walking to the side of the room that had the best view of it, as well as that of the front door, he sat down at the table. He placed a small gold coin, tails up, in the bottom of the bag of chestnuts before the man waiting on him approached his table. When the server did come over to him, Savage ordered a beer.

"Is there anythin else the gentleman might like to have?" asked his server.

"Oh, sure, thanks for askin me, my good fellow!" he exclaimed.

"Wot might that be, Sir?"

"I know Billy in the buttery has a sweet tooth for chestnuts. Will ya give this to im fer me?" the bowman asked. The two statements together meant that he wanted to set up a meeting with Braucus Peredurus.

"I'd be glad to take em to im," came the reply," meaning that the Minister was available to meet with Savage.

"Excellent! You're a good man, now. I look forward to havin the tavern's beer. Heard it's the best around in the port and on the harbor." Savage had told the man he was going to meet the Minister out in the harbor at a predetermined spot.

The server took Savage's order and the bag of chestnuts with him. He did not return to the table. A young boy did, instead. Without saying anything to him, the boy gave the bowman a large tankard of beer and left.

Savage quickly downed his drink and left the tavern. He walked quickly and with purpose this time to an inn that overlooked the bay. He paid for a room for the night, went up to it and made himself at home. Before he settled down for a nap, he wedged the only chair in the room against the door. Eventually, without taking his boots off, he laid down on the rug that was alongside the bed. He got up once to grab one of the two pillows at the head of the bed. He placed it on the floor and stretched back down on it, resting his head on its freshly laundered surface.

He fell asleep quickly. The big man had no dreams.

Upon awakening from his rest, he felt completely refreshed. Savage had the rare ability to awake from a deep sleep without any apparent grogginess. He was optimistic, alert and looking forward to his meeting with the Minister. He knew already what he wanted to say. The rest had helped him prepare for the substance of the meeting, at least on his end of things.

It was dark out. The day's hearty winds had blown all the cloud cover away. There was a clear sky above him with a half–moon shining brightly down onto the city.

Savage walked to the docks by a somewhat circuitous route. He was careful to note if he was being followed or placed under observation. Seeing that everything was clear, he approached a small, locally built boat called a coble. It had a high bow for sailing on the rough waters of the bay. With its open deck, flat bottom, and high bow, it was clinker built, meaning the planks did not overlap one another; they were simply hung on a frame.

The bowman knew the captain of this doughty vessel and that he was highly skilled at maneuvering through the harbor. Without saying much to the captain, except for a brief greeting and exchange of words, Savage was taken to one of the King's naval warships that was anchored further in the bay away from the congestion of ships and boats near the waterfront.

The captain of the coble waited to be sure the big man had successfully started climbing up the ship's ladder to the deck. Seeing that Savage had sprung out from the coble onto the rope ladder with ease, he moved away from the hull of the other ship without even bidding his passenger a farewell and good night.

When savage reached the bulwark of the other ship, the night watchman leaned over and helped give the archer a hand to come on board the deck of the galley. The man drew in a surprised breath at the power of the hand grabbing his own.

As it was a calm night aboard a ship's vessel, The bowman easily adjusted from his land to his sea legs. Another member of the night watch accompanied him to the captain's quarters, which was located underneath the stern deck of the ship.

The watchman knocked politely, but firmly, on the captain's door.

A refined but baritone voice replied, "Come in smartly now!"

The watchman stood back to allow Savage to proceed ahead into the Captain's small, but well-built room.

The big man almost had to double into himself so he could get through the door.

Upon entering the cabin, he saw Braucus Peredurus, the King's Minister of Affairs, standing in back of the captain's desk with a cup of wine in his left hand.

"Welcome, welcome, my friend," he said with a warm spirit of greeting in his voice. "It's been too long since we last met eye to eye with one another. Please, have a seat."

Savage sat down in front of the captain's desk.

The Minister poured a cup of red wine for himself. Looking over at the watchman who was still at the door, he asked, "Everything going according to plan, Sergeant?"

"Aye–aye, Sir. Just the three of us on watch right now. We've got a surface watch going, part of which has four vessels patrolling around the galley, Sir."

"Good, good. The three of you can relax now. Please see to the boat on the starboard side and climb aboard it. I will signal you when you may return. So keep a sharp ear out for it. Understood, Sergeant?"

"Aye–aye, Sir, clear as the bell at noon meal."

The sergeant closed the door softly.

Savage could hear his footsteps walking away. The bowman also heard three pairs of footsteps, along with a muted conversation, proceed to the starboard side of the galley. He heard the boat come alongside the war galley and the watch get on board the tender.

It grew quiet, except for the sounds of the ship moving lightly to the slow swell of the waves lapping at the boat in the midst of the harbor.

The Minister had been listening to his men's departure, too. When all was quiet, he gestured for Savage to sit down and briskly said, "Let's get down to business."

The bowman sat in the chair in front of the captain's desk.

"What's your report cover? Let's see, it's over the last four months, isn't it?"

"Yes, Sir," came the immediate response.

"Here, here. I need to mind my manners. I'm so looking forward to listening to it, I forgot to offer you some wine. My apologies, my friend," said Braucus.

41

"It is excellent wine. It's a red just brought up through the Gasping Sea from the southern tip of Umbria. A courier brought it along with him as he knew I have a predilection for a dry, but full bodied, Cabernet. The black grapes grown in that part of the world are superior to any others of its kind because of the combination of silt, clay, sand and gravel in which the grapes are grown. It's a unique place that gives the grape a special taste you get from no other quarter of any realm."

The Minister poured out the rich looking liquid into a goblet. Handing one to Savage, he toasted the King of West Fündländ, "Here's to our King, long may he reign with grace and power, wisdom and strength."

They raised their drinks to one another and drank deeply from the wine.

"You know, Sir," the bowman said, "if you keep having me drink from your favorite supply of wine, it motivates me to stay in the summer capital and open up a tavern that sells just this quality of wine."

The Minister smiled at Savage's comment. "You're always welcome to join my staff, John. I could use a man like you in this part of the service."

"Yes, you keep offering me such a position, but I still prefer getting out and seeing the world," the archer mused aloud.

"I know; that's what you keep telling me. Yet, I think I detect a weakening resolve in your putting off my offer for you to be at my side near the King's court, no matter where the King takes up residence during the year."

It was the archer's turn to smile, "And, I, Sir, detect a wry comment from you, similar to the Umbrian dust I taste in this wine."

The Minister laughed, "Touché, John! If I promise to keep your cup full, will you promise, in return, to keep your report pouring out of your memory, observations and assessments to what you have observed?"

"Braucus, that's something I have no problem doing for such a liquid and verbal quid pro quo."

Peredurus smiled again, then frowned as he stated, "We have had many raids on the western coast and shores. They are getting stronger in force, duration and predation. We hear that the Western Isles are experiencing the same. But, you can tell me about such matters in a following meeting. King Ealhhere and I sent you out to assess the level of strange events happening throughout the realm. Tell me, are the stories true?"

"I had not directly seen any evidence of out of the ordinary events or their circumstances until the battle that occurred at the field near the source of the Forgotten River. What I observed were strange weather phenomena, unusual activities of animals, birds and unnatural, otherworldly creatures, and heard many men say they had been experiencing strange and violent dreams."

"Besides encountering such, did you also see or hear of anything regarding strange lights, rips in time, or the presence of other spiritual activities?" questioned the Minister.

"Only the latter, your Honor," responded Savage. I came across a young man, a soldier, by the name of Pall Warren. He spells his first name with a double L. At the time I first met him, he did not seem to know who he was, his family background or the context in which he was serving the Realm in the King's northwestern army.

"I suspect that he served in the Aeonian Guard, especially in the style of his uniform, the quality of the sword he carried and how he handled himself in my presence. It is a miracle in itself that he survived the slaughter to the King's troops and to the Guard that was present on the field when the battle took place."

"There was a David Warren who was the High Commander of King Lycidyuse Peredurus' armies. I wonder if this young soldier is a son of the former High Commander," the Minister mused aloud. "Is the sword he carries modeled after a falchion design and double edged?"

"Yes, Sir, that it is."

"How do you rate the quality of the weapon the lad carried?" queried the Minister.

"I would say," Savage speculated, "it is one of the rarest and finest blades I've ever seen, personally."

"We'll examine this curiosity a bit later. What else happened in his presence, John?"

The bowman recounted to the Minister of Affairs all of the strange events that occurred with Pall: the Valravn and its prophecy to the young man, the terrible night at the abandoned farmstead and the battle with the Marauders, as well as the slaughter that occurred, which was unleashed by the three sets of Üngers. He also described the song that Pall sang when one of the Üngers had approached and stalked them in the ale house yard. Last of all, Savage related how a Sentinel Tree had killed an Ünger.

The Minister asked detailed questions about all of these experiences.

Savage answered quickly, astutely and with precision the Minister's follow-up questions.

"May I have permission to speak freely, Minister?" Savage asked.

Peredurus, who had been lightly clasping his hands together and listening intently to Savage's report, simply nodded his head for the bowman to speak.

"Thank you," Savage said. "Since I have been out in the field for this most recent assignment, I have seen an increasing amount of, shall I simply say, mystical events. What used to be considered

45

fictitious or highly fanciful stories, or even a cleric's bald-faced lie, is now something that is occurring on a more regular, factual basis. I'm only one man. And, I have a feeling that other people like me are seeing this rise in uncommon spiritual activity. Is such an assumption correct?"

Again, the Minister nodded his head in affirmation to the archer's question.

"What do you see happening, Braucus?"

The Minister of Affairs unclasped his hands and taking his cup in his right hand, raised it to his lips. He stopped before he took a drink, as if he were going to say something. He took a drink anyway. And then he took another, emptying his goblet. He looked over at Savage, who nodded his head for more.

As Peredurus refilled the archer's goblet and his own, he said, "These types of activities are increasing across the Realm as well as in all those around us. But they seem to be particularly focused in the area where this young man has been. Also, in the same light, so to speak, the Western Isles is reported to have a young woman there who is working miracles never seen for over a thousand years. The High King Peter Áed Menn Rochtmar and his champion, Sir Trevelan du Coeur, have raised her up as a figurehead and symbol for their new campaign against civil unrest there.

"It seems as though major members of the clergy and some in the nobility have taken the raiders in as allies. They are furious over the exploits of this woman called Evangel Blessingvale."

Savage, who was listening intently to the Minister's information, asked, "Were these factions involved in the battle that young Warren was in?"

"Most assuredly, John," was the Minister's reply.

"Was this Blessingvale and her army responsible for the battle Warren was in?"

"On the contrary, John," the Minister responded, "it was an exceptionally strong force of raiders I spoke of earlier."

"Thank you, Braucus. I know you did not have to answer me."

"That's fine, old friend. I know that this information stays with you and you alone. Yet, I think it is important you know the overall context of what is happening. It may be sooner now than later when I will demand your presence by my side to help me better deal with what the King and I are seeing happen in this regard—and with growing alarm and concern, I might add."

"I am at your service. What do you wish for me to do?" Savage asked.

The Minister smiled warmly. "I knew I could count on you. Let's go through what you just shared with me again. Then, I'll give you the details of my new plan and see what you think of it."

Peredurus had Savage repeat his report two more times. More questions followed, and the bowman responded patiently and with as much insight as he could summon to do so.

When his detailed report was through and the Minister's interrogation of the report had ended, they sat in the captain's cabin quietly drinking the exquisite Umbrian Cabernet.

The wooden galley creaked in response to the pull and push of the waves lapping against it. The light of the moon had waned over the time Savage's report to his chief was being given. Still, its illumination on the water sparkled and scattered its rays like diamonds sparkling in their own waves of liquid wealth.

Savage cleared his throat, took another quaff of red wine and stated, "I tracked Gregor Mordant, mostly by guess, conjecture and what I could deduce, to Gullswater. He is either here in Seascale, or he has moved on to parts unknown. To be honest with you, I have a personal score to settle with the man. Can you tell me anything about him?"

The Minister remained quiet for a moment. He sighed and said, "He's off limits to you, John."

"Braucus, don't tell me he's part of your network!" the big man stated bluntly and grimly.

"He's one of the King's handpicked men, and he's of no concern to you at this point in time, no matter your personal vexation with him," the Minister strongly stated.

"You can reprimand me to your heart's desire," the archer insisted, "but my job is to report to you the movements, strength and force displacement of any and all of the King's enemies, or those who choose to oppose him. There's something about Mordant I don't like. I think he's working things according to his own agenda. I'm sensing an over burdensome desire on his part to play false to those using his skills and intelligence networks."

"All right, John," responded the Minister. "I hear the level of professional concern you have over this man; it's duly noted. I'll take it under advisement. In the meantime, you are not going to go near him."

The bowman smiled to himself and thought, *Mordant's here in the port city. Otherwise, I wouldn't have been told to stay away from him.*

"John," cautioned the Minister, "I know what you're thinking. You've got to listen to me on this one. I'll get back to you after I look into it further. In the meantime, keep staying at the place you picked already. Go to the Great Bay Tavern and make it your favorite place to eat and drink. I'll make contact with you in the way we've already set up. I'll also send a small keg of the Cab we're drinking tonight over to the inn at which you're staying if it'll help you keep a low profile."

"Okay, Braucus, I hear you loud and clear," Savage said as he almost stood up straight from his chair. He still had to be careful against banging his head into the ceiling of the captain's cabin.

The Minister stood up as well and smiled at the bowman's discomfit.

They shook hands with one another.

Peredurus led Savage out through the captain's cabin onto the deck. Before he used a belaying pin to knock against the hull of the galley to attract the nearest guard boat to approach the warship, he asked, "What of young Warren? Do you think you will see him again?"

"He was supposed to meet me at a prearranged time, but it was a very conditional plan because of the circumstances surrounding us then."

The Minister leaned over amidships and rapped one end of the belaying pin on the hull sharply. "Is the lad resourceful enough to end up coming here?"

"Aye, my old friend," answered the bowman, "that he most assuredly is already doing even now as we speak.".

CHAPTER SIX

Appropriately, several seagulls overhead cried forlornly as Pall started to walk into the Gullswater Tavern.

Fits my mood exactly, he thought as he glanced up at them. *Wonder if their ancestors were the ones responsible for this place being named after them?*

The young man walked through the front door and approached the owner who was washing down several tabletops.

"May I have a tankard of your best ale, please?" he asked the proprietor.

"Why, surely, sir," came the answer. "Afternoon to you."

The owner turned away from Pall, and shouted over to the kitchen area. "Lawrence, fetch me a tankard of the best ale we've got for this ere gentleman."

He went back to wiping down the surface of another table.

Pall couldn't see the reason why the man was cleaning an already spotless looking tabletop. The table was gleaming as though it was just built, polished to a fine sheen and sent to the tavern for its clients' use.

The owner looked back up at Pall and seemed surprised to see that he was still standing there watching him clean a table. "Look ere, lad, pick a seat. Anyone you like; the boy'll be over to you soon enough. Pay me now, though. I don't trust the boy. I keep im on cause I feel sorry for his ma. His da died last year in a sword fight."

The man went to clean another tabletop. He seemed to forget Pall's presence near him.

Pall went over to the man again, and asked him how much he owed for the ale. The owner told him the amount in a distracted manner. He paid the man and added a generous tip to the price of the ale.

Without looking at the amount of coin Pall had paid him, the proprietor put the money into a small purse that he had taken out of a pocket from his tunic.

The young man walked away from the owner. He stopped and looked around him at the room. Pall decided to take one of the tables at the rear of the room. While he went over to it, he had a brief flashback about being in another tavern, the one in which he encountered the giant Savaric. The recollection went through him with an intensity that almost knocked him to the tavern floor.

He mentally tore the memory away from his mind. To help give a finality of ripping it away, he shook himself like a dog coming out of the water. Droplets of his companions' voices, and the riddling challenges he and the giant traded with one another, scattered away from him.

He looked over at the four customers who were scattered throughout the room, but none of them seemed to be paying any attention to him. No sooner had he sat down Lawrence came over and served him his ale. Pall thanked the boy and waited for him to leave his table.

Again, Pall looked at the customers in the room. He wondered if he should go talk to them now about whether or not they had seen or heard of Savage being in Gullswater. He shook his head in frustration. *I guess it'll have to wait for a better time.*

He decided to relax. Tension, built up in him since the day he walked off the field of battle, and then first met Savage, started draining away. He drank deeply from his cup of ale and became lost in thought.

To his surprise, and what seemed but a moment later, he opened his eyes and saw that Lawrence was at his table. The boy had asked him a question, which Pall had not heard.

The boy smirked at him and mimed if Pall wanted another drink.

Pall looked dourly at the tavern boy and pushed the tankard over to him, signing back that he wanted another drink.

Lawrence took the empty flagon and soon brought back a freshly refilled one.

Pall, not wanting to keep the signing going between them said, "Thank you, I'll be sure to pay the owner when he comes by me."

Lawrence shrugged his shoulders to indicate that he didn't care and left Pall's company.

Without taking a sip of his second drink, Pall fell back into his reverie of blank abstraction.

Lawrence came back two more times with new drinks on each occasion.

Pall fell asleep at the table on his fourth tankard of ale.

Around him, the tables slowly became occupied and the room filled up with local customers. They looked at his battle worn clothes, his sword sheathed by his side and the tiredness in his expression. When they looked at his hands that had dropped open on his lap, they saw the calluses and the history of a soldier's training in them.

Everyone decidedly left the young man alone.

A hand suddenly fell on his left shoulder. Thinking that he was tied up and Mustard was again tormenting him in the farmhouse, Pall reached out with his right hand to stop being touched. People watching him saw a young man somehow grab the other man's wrist, slide out of the chair he was sitting in and duck under the other man's arm all at once, but in a blur of action. The young soldier was a blink of an eye from breaking his supposed opponent's wrist and forearm.

"Pall, Pall, it's me. You're okay. I was just going to say hello to you. It's okay," said the man.

Pall stopped the deadly momentum he was about to bring to bear on this stranger.

"Hey, it's all right. I wasn't trying to be rude. Even stupid to get you angry. I...."

Pall realized in a sudden rush that Merek was standing in front of him. The young soldier reversed his grip and locked his hand on Merek's forearm.

"Merek!" he exclaimed. "It's you! You're alive!"

Merek laughed loudly, "Yep, it sure is me. No monster gonna get me that easy, even though I thought we were both gone with it chasin after us so. I don't know that it would have stuck around us so much if you had put your hand on it the way you did to me just now!"

Pall laughed a bit uncomfortably.

Seeing that Pall recognized a friend and not a foe, Merek relaxed a bit more saying, "Well now, you're a sight for bleedin eyes! What have you been up to and why are you here?"

"I'm trying to find Savage," the young soldier responded. "We were supposed to meet him where he told us that night at the farmstead. But Ünger changed those plans when he came after us."

Merek watched his friend stop offering an explanation and then stare out at something only Pall could see. To divert his mood from going sour to worse than morbid, Merek quickly broke into Pall's statement.

"I talked to a lot of people on the road to Gullswater. They never saw anything close to lookin like Ünger. They thought I was mad or somethin cause they didn't want to talk about it. A couple of people in town here said they saw the big man. But he was just passin through and very quickly at that."

Both men had sat down at Pall's table. Lawrence came by and served them another drink. While he took their order, the boy kept warily looking at Pall, as though he was expecting to be hit by him.

Merek noticed the boy's reticence. "It's all right, lad. My friend here's harmless as a baby toad."

Lawrence looked at Merek as though he had said something truly ludicrous. The boy literally ran away from the table.

Laughing, Pall said, "I think you made it worse. He might not even come back with our drinks."

"That's all right, I'll go get em if I have to and I'll apologize to the boy," Merek offered.

Realizing what Merek had told him concerning the whereabouts of Savage, Pall asked, "Do you know why Savage was here in Gullswater?"

"That I do," answered the man once named Twin, "just as I now know that the name Gullswater came from a single bird of its kind that was blown inland from a great storm. When the founders of the town arrived here, they couldn't believe they were seeing an ocean bird on a freshwater river."

"Thanks for the history lesson, Merek. But how did you know about Savage?" insisted Pall.

"Because the people I spoke with about him told me about some of the town's history," he responded with some irritation.

"Okay," Pall said back to him. He patiently asked, "So did these same folks tell you why the bowman was here to begin with?"

"Yep!" Merek infuriatingly acknowledged.

"And?" Pall urged, trying to coax a fuller explanation out of his friend.

Merek studied his left wrist where Pall had first grabbed him. He looked up at Pall and smiled half disparagingly. "He's gone after Gregor Mordant."

Any remnant of sleepiness and lethargy remaining in him was swept away upon hearing this news from Merek. Questions started coming to his mind. "Why does Savage want to go after Mordant?"

"I'm not sure, but I think I've got an answer to that question," Merek answered.

"Which is...?" queried Pall.

"Mordant's not simply what he appears to be on the surface. He's a very complicated sort. As the leader of the Marauders, he gets to raise hell with everything around him. And, he loves his 'job'. You can tell by how he's so enthusiastic having us going about everywhere he sends us pillaging, raping, burning, destroying, torturing, stealing, selling stuff illegally…. Well, you get what I mean. But he himself, personally, participates in doing all of these things and with all of his heart, too."

Pall interrupted Merek by asking, "So what's so special about Mordant that would have someone like Savage on his trail? Why would Mordant's activities cause Savage to hunt for him? Is it something personal between them?"

"Whoa, my interrogator, one question at a time!" Merek said. "Gregor Mordant happens to be not just an outlaw. He uses his 'occupation' as a Marauder as a mask for doing something else."

Merek went quiet after making this last statement.

With a frustration that fairly approached a seething level, Pall urged, "Go on, Merek, quit playing the dramatic games with me. I've had enough morality plays from you to last me a lifetime or three. Make some sense to why Mordant is being marked by Savage."

Merek sighed deeply. "Okay, here it is. My opinion. The truth about my former leader. He's former, right, because I was already sick of leading the kind of life I had following him. When Carac was killed by that thing that was after us, something broke in me. I never want to return to that awful way of living. Watching and being a part of torturing you also made me realize it wasn't who I wanted to be. Please forgive me for doing what I did to you."

"It's okay, Merek, you've already apologized to me. Don't worry about such things. Please tell me why you think Savage wants to find Mordant."

Merek took a deep breath and let it out slowly. He inhaled a big gulp of air and said, "I blame Mordant for my brother's death. Anything I can do to help get him turned into the authorities, or simply just destroyed, I want to help do so. But turning him into the authorities won't help stop him."

"Why, Merek?"

"Because he's part of them," he said.

When Pall looked blankly at him, Merek added, "He's part of the authorities. Cause he's a spy for the King."

"How do you know this for a fact?" Pall asked with great curiosity.

"Mordant used to send Error all around to do his bidding for him. Error would have me and my brother helping him a lot. We used to spy on the King's troop movements and do everything we could to falsify the information being sent to the King. We helped other raiders come into this land and raid our own people. We helped make people angry and we recruited people to act out against the King."

"This is why you think Savage went after him?"

"Yes, Pall, because Savage has to work for the Realm, too, except he's loyal to the King; Mordant's not cause he's a traitor. That's why he's after my Commander, I mean former Commander."

Savage works for the King! He thought.

Pall could see that Merek's comment about Savage made complete sense and helped fill in the gaps about Savage's wanderings and knowledge about things happening around him.

The young soldier looked steadily at Merek for a moment. "How are you going to get your revenge against Mordant?"

"By finding him," Merek conjectured, "you'll also find Savage because he won't be far behind em. Because I know where most of the Marauder leadership meets with its connections, associates, spies and paid informants. I know their codes and secret places of meeting."

"Merek, you mean to tell me that you can take me to find Savage?"

The former Marauder did not directly answer Pall's question. Instead, he made the following claim, "If and when Mordant arrived here in Gullswater, he wouldn't stay here long at all. He would try to get away in less than a day. He would go to Seascale on the Forgotten River."

"How do you know this?"

"I know it because he would've gone to a man named Moro Asutuo to get a boat to Seascale. Error, me and my brother used to go meet Asutuo for similar reasons. This man Moro is the chief spy for this part of the Kingdom. He works for Mordant directly. He helped get a boat for Gregor so's he could go to Seascale on the Forgotten River."

"Merek," Pall asked hopefully, "do you have a way we can find Mordant?"

"Yes, I do. I think it's a good one, too. We go to Moro's place on the river and have him get us a boat as well. I know of at least two possible places where Mordant will be in the port city. We'll go there and find him."

"What are you going to do when you find Mordant?"

"Why, have you told Savage where Mordant is staying?" he asked with a gleam in his eyes.

CHAPTER SEVEN

Merek and Pall agreed to meet one another again in the tavern later on that night, halfway between dusk and the midnight hour. They left the tavern and went their separate ways. Merek went to Moro's place. Pall went to Tom's new home.

It was getting later on in the afternoon. The strength of the sun's light was waning, while the heat of the day was still building towards an oppressive weight. Merek found himself sweating profusely. He couldn't tell whether or not he was perspiring because he was uncomfortably hot, or if he was just overly uncomfortable about what he had set out doing in trying to find the Commander.

Must be a little bit of both, he thought.

Reaching the waterfront where Moro's broken-down shack was located, he drew near the damaged front door. No one appeared to be around, but Merek knew that was just for appearance. He understood that he was being watched the whole time.

Probably watched even at the tavern and now followed here, with Asutuo knowing every step I've made.

He knocked on the door with his left hand set of knuckles three distinct times. The first set was five raps, the second was four, and the final one was five again, but the loudest of the three.

He waited at the front door as if his patience were about to fray on the spot. While doing so, he placed the sole of his left foot on a small piece of charcoal. Along with acting increasingly impatient, he scuffed his boot four times and left a small "W" on the granite threshold before the door.

Merek waited another forty heartbeats, appearing to be hopeful someone was imminently going to respond to his presence. No one did.

He left the front of the shack looking dejected, if not downright forlorn.

He retraced his steps to the Gullswater Tavern where he went into the back entrance. Going up one flight of wooden stairs, he entered a hallway to a set of rented rooms. He found his own and let himself in.

The only surviving twin in his family took off his boots and threw himself down on the bed. Looking up at the ceiling, he thought of his brother dying a hideous death by the Ünger. He again saw Pall's suffering at the hands of Gordo, his brother and himself. He worked himself up into a passion of anger and profound revenge.

If an astute observer had been in the room, he would have noticed that before Merek closed his eyes, there was a gleam back in them.

Pall sweated his way back to Tom's. He was relieved to know that Merek had survived Ünger's presence when they had separated from one another in the woods in order to divide the monster's attention away from at least one of them. Pall went cold at the realization that the demon could have split itself into three. He did not understand why that had not occurred.

Perhaps the creature was just too overconfident and greedy for consuming another man, he considered.

He then speculated where the other two Üngers had gone. *I wonder if there are more than two others walking around? Could there be a race of them? Everything in the world consists of multiple copies of the same creatures. Ants, deer, mocking birds, trout, mosquitos, spiders, people: why not Üngers as well? Certainly, there are other evil things present in our world, too. Like the Valravn....*

Pall looked up and noticed that he had arrived at Tom's place. He went to the front entrance of the cooper's shop. As it was so hot, the door was wide open. He knocked on the side of the door frame.

Myra answered from inside, "Who is it?"

"It's me, Myra, Pall."

The next thing he knew, a three-year-old child was running as fast as she could towards him. She jumped at him upon reaching him. He caught her in midair with his arms and gave her a big bear hug.

When she stopped hugging him, she reared back and looked at him in mock anger. "Where have you been, Pilgrim?" she asked.

"Exploring, little one," he answered with a grin. "What have you been doing?"

"I've been helping Da work," she said with great self-importance.

"Oh, that is important," the young soldier responded, "because I don't think he could do it without your help."

Myra looked at him closely to see if he was being serious. "No, I'm just little. Da's just trying to make me feel better. He can do everything by himself anyways."

It was Pall's turn to look at her with some scrutiny. "You know, child," he said to her, "we've talked about this before. Your da needs you, and you need him. You may be little, but you carry a giant's weight in helping your da work."

Not completely understanding his meaning, she asked, "How can a little girl like me, without a mother and sister now, help my da?"

Pall carried her inside the door into the shop. Tom was in the front room listening to their conversation with one another.

Pall looked at the little girl's father and back at her. Smiling gently at her, he said, "Because you give him hope. And without hope he would be lost."

"Really?" she asked.

"Really, Pilgrim," he responded.

She laughed as he put her down on the shop's wooden floor. Myra ran over to her father, who, in turn, picked her up in his arms.

Tom looked over at Pall and said knowingly, "You're leaving us."

Pall nodded soundlessly.

"Right now?" the cooper asked him.

"Yes, Tom."

Tom walked over to Pall. With Myra still in the cooper's competent arms, they hugged the young warrior. Tom stood back and said, "You know that you will always have a place here if you need it."

Pall nodded his head. He could not say anything at that moment.

"You find what you were lookin for?"

"Yes," he barely was able to say.

Tears were streaming down Tom Cooper's face. His daughter, looking stricken at the sight of them falling away from his eyes, touched them as they fell.

Pall put his right hand on Tom's left shoulder. He touched Myra on the side of her face. He turned around and left the cooper's shop. Before going out the door, his own tears fell as well. They hit his hands as he was walking through it. They hit the door's wooden threshold. They hit the stone pathway to Tom and Myra's new home. They hit deeply into the very center of his sense of wellbeing.

The young man felt that he was leaving his home.

At nine o'clock that night, Pall joined Merek at one of the tables in the Gullswater Tavern. They ordered food and drinks. Lawrence would not take their order. The tavern keeper did.

"What did you do or say to the boy?" he asked them.

"I'm not sure what you mean," Merek responded.

"Lawrence won't come near you. Says you scared him to death."

"I am truly sorry that I have set the lad back off his feet," Pall responded. "I acted without thinking when my friend met me here earlier in the day. I think Lawrence expects me to do the same with him."

Looking mollified with Pall's answer, the proprietor said, "Aye, thank you for that. It's kind of you to admit fault. Brave, too. Not many men like you would do so. The lad, well, he's skittish when it comes to bein around men with swords."

The owner walked away quickly, and as quickly as he left, their order was brought back to them by another, older server.

Both men dug into their food. They did not exchange any words with one another. They were brought two square wooden plates that exhibited a very primitive form of workmanship. On the top of the plate was a thick slice of tavern made bread. On the bread was a thicker slice of pork dripping with gravy. The rim of the plate had a small hollow space that contained salt for their meat. They applied the salt without tasting their food first.

They ate as though they had not done so in a great while and were not going to eat again for an even longer period next. Finishing their meal, they flipped their wooden plates over as this indicated that the other side of the plate could be used for another course.

Lawrence approached their table with some trepidation, but he took their plates back to the kitchen nevertheless. Soon he reappeared with them. They were heaped with steaming vegetables, and more of the gravy that had been served with the pork, upon another thick slice of bread.

It was not long before the vegetables, gravy and bread had been heartily eaten.

Merek belched loudly, making an obvious show of appreciation for the meal he and Pall had practically inhaled in a very short amount of time. He kicked Pall unobtrusively under the table. Taking the hint, Pall also burped appreciatively and smacked his lips in delight of having the food, which was not hard to do because it was truly excellently prepared and cooked.

When Lawrence returned to take their plates away, Merek ordered another round of drinks for themselves. He told the lad, "Lawrence, thank you for serving us. It's good to see you again. Would you be a kind lad and bring the gentleman all alone at the table on my right a drink of ale as well?"

The boy gave a hint of a smile, nodded his head and went immediately away from the table.

Three drinks were brought back. Lawrence served Merek and Pall and then he served Moro the third.

Finishing their drinks, Merek paid for their meals. They stood up from their table. As Merek walked by Moro, he briefly nodded at him.

Asutuo seemed not to pay any attention to the two men walking by him, despite the fact that they had bought him a drink. He had his left hand wrapped around the base of the cup and was looking at it with studied intent.

They walked towards the tavern door.

The owner came over to them as they reached it. "Thank you for your patronage," he said. "And thank you for being kind to my nephew."

Merek nodded at the man.

Pall said with sincerity, "The food and ale were delicious. Thank you for treating us so well."

The owner bobbed his head in delight and said, "God's speed to you gentlemen."

"To you as well, Sir," replied Merek.

Walking onto the street from the tavern, Pall was about to say something to Merek, who in the light of the doorway saw that his companion wanted to speak. Merek touched Pall's elbow lightly and shook his head to stop him from saying anything.

Pall followed Merek's lead. They took a roundabout way back to Moro's dilapidated shack. The moon was half full and provided enough light for them to navigate their way in the dark to the river front. Instead of approaching the place from the street side, Merek took them around the back of the building on the river's side of it. He and Pall entered the building from that direction.

They walked into a dimly lit hallway and almost immediately heard the sound of a door squeak open. As they approached closer to it, they could see an inconstant, fitful light illumined the interior room. Passing through the opening, they observed Moro seated at a table, which was overburdened with paper, manuscripts, writing utensils and a set of throwing knives that glistened wickedly in the flickering candlelight. The candle had almost burned itself out.

"Buona sera, amico," greeted Moro.

"Buona sera, Capo," returned Merek.

Asutuo extinguished the remaining stub of the lit candle with the thumb and index finger of his left hand. As soon as he did so, moonlight filled the room. They followed him outside the building and to a small rowboat tied off an equally small pier on the river.

Merek stepped into the skiff and sat in the prow of the boat. Pall sat in the middle.

With practiced ease and agility, Moro got in the boat and stepped into its stern. He and Merek released the stern and spring lines. Soon, the man known as "the dark one" was seated and powerfully rowing the boat upstream.

Moro swiftly brought them to their destination, whereupon he and Merek secured the boat to another small pier. Once secured, they stepped out of the skiff onto the landing.

Moro led them up a white graveled path to his home. Entering the house, he lighted several candles. He invited both men to sit at the table that was in the room. The dark one poured out three drinks of red wine, serving Merek, Pall and then himself.

"I have made sure," he informed Merek, "that Captain Eumero will give you and your companion passage on his boat *La Signora Maria* to Seascale."

"Grazie, Capo."

"Non parlarne, amico," purred the dark man reassuringly. "It was good of you both to treat

Lawrence tonight with the kindness you showed him, and to talk with his uncle as humbly as you did, as well."

"Famiglia è importante, Capo. Senza di essa siamo perduti."

Looking at Pall intently, Moro responded in English to Merek's comment. "Yes, family is important. We are lost without it, wouldn't you agree?"

Pall looked back steadily at Asutuo and responded, "Without a doubt, it is the anchor that keeps us moored safely in the ocean of life."

The dark one nodded his head in appreciation of Pall's statement, saying, "Questo è innegabilmente vero!" Moro looked over at Merek for his response.

"My companion speaks an undeniable truth, Capo," he affirmed.

Satisfied with the words they had exchanged with him, Moro informed them, "We will rise at dawn tomorrow morning."

They finished their drinks and bid their host goodnight. The two young men stood up from the table when Moro did likewise. After Moro left the room with one of the candles to seek his evening's rest, Merek pointed out a room to Pall where he could sleep. He handed Pall the second candle while he took the remaining one.

Both men went to their separate rooms and soon were asleep in the rough cots that were available for them to use.

Morning came early. Moro woke them well before first light appeared. Taking up a lantern and lighting it, he made sure that its light was shuttered on three sides. The fourth was open partially and allowed them to see where they were walking on the graveled path leading back to the river.

The Captain was already there in his longboat.

Moro said, "The Captain will take excellent care of you and see you safely to your destination in the port city. Please be sure to give my salutations to the Commander, amico."

"I will gladly do so, Capo. Grazie."

Moro nodded his head at Merek.

The men got on board.

The dawn's first light broke open upon them.

Captain Eumero approached Merek and Pall, greeting them heartily. After doing so, he returned to the stern of the longboat and made sure that they disembarked properly from the pier.

The two young men went to the port side of the boat. As they moved downstream, they watched the figure of Asutuo diminish and soon disappear.

Merek looked at Pall and softly whispered to him, "While it went well with Mordant's chief agent, I think he's suspicious of us. Something set him off."

In the same sotto voice, Pall responded, "He saw my sword."

Merek nodded. "We need to be very careful as we approach the port city. Captain Eumero could dump us in the river just before we get there."

Pall nodded. His right hand reached over and firmly gripped the hilt of the sword forged and expertly shaped out of a strange, foreign metal for him by his father. As the longboat went swiftly around a bend in the river, he heard his father singing and praying over the sword as David Warren painstakingly hammered the blade into its deadly form for the fourth and final time.

CHAPTER EIGHT

Seascale was a beautiful place to be. The Commander reveled in being there. Built on top of a natural limestone promontory, its one hundred five–foot sloping walls were made up of the finest quality limestone. The top of the parapets was up to twenty–five feet wide, the base being half more in its width and extending another twelve levels below ground. Mordant often would spend time walking these walls, talking with the guards posted on them and looking out at the Great Bay beyond them.

He knew that the stone he walked upon was quarried from the other side of the crescent shaped bay. Ages ago, it had been brought by barge to the location where he now stood and built with great skill by the architects and masons of that ancient time. When the sun threw its light on the walls themselves, he thought it seemed to caress them as a lover touches his paramour. As a result of the sun's fervor on the stone's clear surface, the walls responded in a light golden yellow blush.

The Commander, like many others who surveyed them, often was awed at the size of not only the heft and girth of the stones, but the incredible manner in which they were set one upon, and in alignment with, the other. Many of them averaged out between four to ten tons apiece. For every three hundred foot span of the wall, he could see stones measuring out to thirty feet in length and weighing as much as three hundred and forty tons. There was one great stone set at each of the four cardinal compass points. These stones were, on average, fifty feet in length and weighed five hundred and seventy tons apiece.

The secrets of working with these huge blocks of building materials were gone from memory. The ancient mastery of working with stones had been forgotten. They died with the original builders. Some thought that only magic of a special kind could have been used to do so. The stones fit so well together that a sharp knife blade could not fit between them. Designs were carved into them, as well as seats, statues in bass relief and stairs. The combination of their age and the weathering on them had removed any tool marks that would have remained otherwise.

The stone, originating from the Great Bay Quarry, was called by the ancient stonemasons "Emperor's Stones," or "Standfast Stones." These craftsmen could cut them like cheese out of the quarry where the very ground had formed them there. As they aged, they hardened to the strength of marble. A cult had even formed to worship them and to see that their implacable, immoveable and obdurate qualities continued to protect the city from any attack, be it originating from economic, military or spiritual origins.

The city's defenses had never been breached in their long and storied history.

Since his arrival in Seascale on *The Lady Mary*, the Commander believed that he had spent his time here productively. He had set up and primed his intelligence networks. He had communicated with the key members of the non–priestly and non–aristocratic classes, those every day, ordinary people who did not belong with the entrenched military, religious or royal echelons sympathetic to the Crown.

He had set the web of his organization to include, for example, the victualers, who purchased the agricultural goods flowing in and out of the city. Thus, key individuals, sympathetic to his cause, were told to be alert to his orders. Those who turned these goods into consumable food, such as the brewers, the bakers and the butchers, were also made aware of his desire to measure the pulse of the city.

Merchants involved in exporting and importing durable goods were contacted for the same purposes. Those who made textiles, metal, wood and military products, including weapons and armor, were specifically added to his list of watchers.

Men and women who sold their skills and services were approached as well. Clerks, prostitutes, accountants, and freight haulers were used to pay heed to the daily course of their businesses. He avoided the entertainers.

"I do not trust those that spread stories," he became well known to many working for him for saying. "Their kind is more fickle than those who spread their legs. I rely more on those who wag their tales than those repeating them."

Mordant, in the brief amount of time spent to date in the port city, had not only made contact with his network chiefs, he was well on his way in colluding with the conservative members of the nobility and clergy in West Fündländ. Contact with these two groups of people in other realms, such as the Western Isles, was made by men like Captain Eumero.

Before he returned to Gullswater to speak with the dark one there, Eumero was curious as to why Mordant was so bent on getting his espionage and intelligence networks at a fever pitch in alertness.

"Tell me, Commander," he said one night when the two were on board his longboat, "are you going to war with someone?"

Mordant, deep in thought, did not respond at once. He was drinking the ale Eumero had poured for the both of them. Gregor was enjoying the moment. He liked being on the water, even if *La Signora Maria* was tied up at one of his merchant friend's wharfs.

He looked out at the city, whose lights sparkled on the surface of the harbor around the longboat.

The ripple of water from the incoming tide pushed the hull of the boat gently against the wooden side of the wharf. The sound of wood responding to the flow of the ocean's current soothed his uneasiness.

Eumero refilled their cups and waited patiently for Mordant to answer him. He had given most of the men on his crew the evening off. Only two men were on duty and they were posted at both ends of the dock from where the longboat was berthed. Eumero made sure that they stayed out of the hearing range of his and the Commander's low–pitched voices.

Mordant looked at the Captain and remarked, "Thank you for tolerating my agitation, my friend. To answer your question…," he paused and took a drink from his cup, "not only are we at war already, but certain forces in the Kingdom, and those surrounding us, are beginning to resist our efforts at destabilizing Ranulf's control of his realm."

Eumero held back his questions, remaining quiet in hopes of hearing the Commander explain his thoughts more fully, if not more candidly, instead.

"Something happened to me and my men at a farmhouse in the forest within three to four hours walk to the battlefield where our raiders attacked the King's elite Aeonian Guard."

Again the Commander paused. Although he couldn't see the ale in his cup, he stared into it anyway, as though the surface of the liquid was a scrying device able to tell him the secrets he wanted to know more about and was trying to share with the Captain.

The Captain refilled Gregor's cup.

"We left the Gullswater Road to raid and ruin this farm. At first, we figured no one was there. Error and I thought someone else, or another group of our men, had gotten there before us. There were no animals, no signs of the farmer and his family. Yet, tools had been left outside in places as though something had interrupted those working with them.

"Some of the men found a young man about to enter the farmhouse. They took him inside. Error, then myself, questioned him. We didn't get anywhere with him. He seemed not himself. So, we hogtied him and let Gordon play with him for the remainder of the night, thinking that it would loosen the lad's tongue."

Mordant stopped his narrative and gave a frustrated sigh.

Eumero could not help himself and asked, "What is it, Commander? Who was this young man?"

"He was a nobody. Yet, he carried himself like a leader and he spoke in a well–educated, aristocratic tongue. But the truly interesting aspect about him, at least at first, was he carried with him one of the most uncommon sword blades I have ever seen."

"Perhaps he took it from the battlefield, or killed someone from there who first had stolen it," offered the captain of the longboat.

"That crossed our minds, but we rejected it because of the man's deportment. Like I said, Error and I were going to treat him rough and see what we could get from him the next morning. We never got a chance to question him further."

"Why, what happened?"

"During the middle of the third watch, one of the Thaumaturge's creatures went berserk and attacked my men."

"How could this happen? I thought such a thing was impossible!" exclaimed Eumero.

"So did we," confirmed Mordant. "It is worse than I am telling you. The creature reached its maximum threat level and split into nine entities. They attacked every man among us. The lad they left alone."

"These matters, indeed, prove quite disturbing. What is another one that causes you to set our networks on a complete war footing?"

Gregor took several pulls from his mug. "One of the tallest and one of the most dangerous of men I know was also there. He was killing my men with great abandon alongside the nine Üngers."

Eumero swore softly. "If I did not know you for over twenty years, I would not believe such a tale."

The Commander laughed. "Yes, Captain, and even now as I am telling you this experience, I find it hard to believe as well."

"But, it's true, nevertheless?" Eumero queried, hoping the man opposite him was joking, or only exaggerating the issue he had just related to him.

"Yes, as true as the fact both of us are on your longboat drinking your ale and talking with one another at night in this harbor."

"Who was the big one fighting you and your Marauders?" Eumero asked as he took a drink from his cup of ale.

"The bowman, John Savage."

The Captain choked on his drink, coughed repeatedly and got up from where he had been seated on the midship rail. He leaned over the starboard side and spat what he could not swallow from his drink into the sea.

"I'd join you if I could, Captain, but your ale is too good to puke over the side of the railing."

Gregor's humor made the Captain cough, spit and gasp some more. Catching some of his equilibrium back, Eumero said in a hoarse voice, "You seem to be taking this in stride, no?"

"No, Captain, I just was enjoying making you seem seasick and watching you act as though you never had your sea legs."

Eumero walked up and down the deck of his ship twice, the first time to get his gorge down from choking on the ale, while the second was his attempt to think on his feet about what Mordant had just revealed to him.

The Captain walked up to Gregor and asked, "Is this John Savage the same as one of the King's intelligence lieutenants who works hand in hand with Braucus Peredurus?"

"Aye, Captain, one and the same he is."

"Did he see you at the farmhouse?"

"No, not at first, although he saw me in the moonlight at that abandoned farmhouse. He may have been the one who killed the farmer and his family, or he and the Ünger may have done so together. I don't really care which did which; the result was the same."

"Did he follow you?"

"Yes, Captain, I would expect no less of a man such as him to do so."

"But, you obviously eluded him, Commander."

"Only for the moment and temporarily at best, Captain Eumero."

"So, you have been contacting all our people because of Savage?"

"Not only, yet assuredly, he has spoken with the Minister of Affairs, who is already vetting Savage's report. Peredurus is no vacillating toady of the King's. Even though it will take some time to do so, the Minister will stir the pot subtly and vigorously. I have felt compelled to push our time table up ahead of schedule."

"Thus, Commander, your wanting everyone on the alert for Savage's whereabouts?"

"Aye, Eumero, and for having the full force of the invasion break upon this decadent realm sooner than we planned."

"What do you plan to do with the bowman, then?" asked Eumero.

Mordant refilled both their cups, raised his high in the air and toasted, "Why, bring the big fly into our web here in Seascale!" he exclaimed heartily.

The two men clanged their mugs against one another and drank deeply from them.

The thaumaturge Gregor Mordant had referred to in his conversation with Captain Eumero was an ultra–radical member of the clergy. Along with Moro Asutuo in Gullswater, this priest was an astute practitioner in the dark arts. He came from the far south where, as an abbot, he abandoned his monastery. The monastery was a traditional one that was rent asunder by the trouble not only caused by this apostate priest, but by his violent and scurrilous attacks on those members of the monastery and clergy not agreeing with his dissent, disobedience and defiance of church doctrine.

Taking well over half of the monks and priests there with him, he fled to the north. Along the way, in every place he journeyed through, he caused controversy, dissension and a falling out amongst members of the conservative Mother Church. Yet, his brilliance and passion as an orator, his startling good looks and outstanding physical condition, including his intelligence and commitment to the doctrine he espoused, won over many converts to his side.

When he reached the port city, he set himself and his followers up in an abandoned monastery outside the city walls. He had over three hundred adherents and devotees with him at the time he first set foot in this large, deserted clerical estate. He had been ensconced there for almost twelve years. Throughout those years, he continued to attract many others to his monastic order. His following now numbered almost twice the amount of members he started with when he initially arrived in Seascale.

The general population, even the nobility, aristocracy and the Crown, considered him an asset to the city. With his oversight, vision, and plans for restoring and remodeling the monastery, he had built it into a work of art. He was given permission by the King to use any stones he could carve out and carry from the old quarry where the city's walls had been taken. His men had worked in the quarry for a decade, such that, they had rebuilt the old monastery's walls and buildings so that they shone in a similar fashion to those Emperor's Stones on Seascale's fortified defense walls.

The monastery had the finest hospital in the north. They trained the best doctors of medicine and these men were sought after by many throughout the land and by many suffering people from foreign lands as well. It also had set up guilds in the trades, agricultural, mercantile and manufacturing professions. Key members of the monastery had been given apostolic powers and sent out to all lands to preach the gospel of the Church of Equity. These men assigned apostles and founders to start churches and to build other monasteries throughout the areas where their preaching took root and created hundreds of followers in turn.

Members of the Church of Equity adopted a seemingly benign symbol to represent their beliefs and to recognize one another wherever they happened to live or travel. It looked as follows:

תרור

The creation, building and maintaining of other churches grew at an exponential rate, such that two other parallel movements were started. These religious movements also attracted more followers and disciples. The House of Martyrs, with its complementary logo of

मु३ो डर,

was established, as was the Sanctuary of Splendor, whose symbol became

τρόμου.

Only a handful of his followers, consisting of all priests, knew that these symbols stood for the words terror, dismay and dread. Despite the irony of this fact, their tattooed popularity sparked a wide-ranging spate of graffiti found throughout the world, as well as in the coded messages sent throughout their ever–growing networks.

Kosem Mungadai was a thaumaturge of the 13th level in the occult arts.

The depth, power and corruption of his arcane knowledge were situated squarely within the realm of demonic summoning. While he preached peace to the world, he sowed and reaped discord, hate and war. To the public he performed great feats of miraculous healing. His displays of magical powers in the forums of the cities he visited were stunning achievements of his "piety" and "goodness".

Certainly, many thought, *the hand of God is upon him.*

Mungadai had become so popular, his reach into the minds of many so pervasive, that he was appointed to be the cleric for the consortium of raiders and foreign interests that had been causing much unrest throughout the northern half of the world. His sole goal was the absolute destruction of all realms, as well as the eradication of what he referred to as "subsidiary religions", everywhere his imprimatur and dispensation reached.

He wanted to release an additional movement and to establish a Temple of Wonder that would be the capital seat for the surrounding territory of each former realm he conquered. Its symbol was already created and looked as shown below:

恐怖

Since Mordant's arrival in Seascale, he had been staying on the grounds at the monastery of the Church of Equity. Gregor was fascinated, mortified, awed and repelled by Kosem Mungadai. He had known the charismatic priest for the full twelve years Mungadai had been in the port city. It was Mordant who helped the priest find the abandoned monastery, and it was Mordant who was the prime mover in having the King grant permission for the place to be given over to the cleric.

Moro Asutuo was one of the original three hundred followers who had settled in Seascale with the renegade priest. He had even been with Mungadai in the far south when the priest had taken his disciples with him to the far northern realms.

It was through Mungadai and Asutuo that the Commander was put in touch with Prioress Matasan and Abbot Athdar of the Western Isles. These two members of the clergy were playing pivotal roles in spreading the Mungadai doctrine of dissension in High King Peter Áed Menn Rochtmar's kingdom.

Mordant and Asutuo had visited both clerics at their respective holdings of St. Åyrwyus Priory and Dawn's Abbey. They had stayed a month with them, two weeks each, for their initial visit. Asutuo had gone back to the Western Isles to solidify the spiritual gains made there. It was being arranged that Mungadai would be giving them an official state visit the following year, which was blessed by the respective clergy in both realms. Even the two kings of each kingdom had communicated with one another over this plan to have the priest visit High King Rochtmar and his wife, the High Queen Isolde Bébhinn Menn Rochtmar.

As Mordant and Eumero toasted one another's plans, Mungadai was in his monastery consulting with his spiritual guides. He traditionally did this in a room that he had specially built for this augury. It was in the lowest level of the monastery, beneath the buttery. Dug out of the rough limestone upon which the building was set, was a square room, ten feet to a side. Affixed against the four stone walls were mirrors that ran the full height and width of each wall.

Only the priest entered this room and did so by descending into it with a ladder that was let down from the ceiling. Upon reaching the floor of the divination room, he could raise the ladder and close himself off from the rest of the monastery and the world. Vents had been built into the ceiling that allowed for fresh air to circulate throughout the enclosure.

In the middle of the room was a large, concentric stone that rested upon a square stone plinth made out of obsidian. Hollowed out in the center, it held water into which the priest would gaze at the ceiling, which also had a mirrored surface. The stone holding the water was five feet in circumference. It was made of black marble containing silvery streaks of white that seemed to shift in the wavering light of candles. Sometimes images would form, places from other worlds and dimensions could be seen in it. Looking at them through the refraction of the water seemed to add a depth to it that made it appear as a portal into these recondite vistas.

The priest would fast a day and then take a hallucinogenic drink before entering the room naked. He would spend one to three days in it depending upon the length of the communication that he could achieve with the chthonic powers he contacted. The darknesses speaking to him revealed themselves in various forms. Depending who deigned to visit with him, sometimes animal, fish, bird, man or woman descended upon him from the mirror on the ceiling and appear before him as summoned. Often, they would merge with one another into malign concoctions of therianthropic creatures. Half human and half animal specters would cavort in malevolent glee around him, taunting him with irreverent and obscene comments and gestures. On occasion, they would not visibly appear, but whisper to him in the dark tongues of implication, analogy, and gruesome metaphor.

In a foreign, guttural tongue, he called them by their names, such as *nightmare*, *dream*, *violent death*, *deceit*, *madness*, *vengeance*, *blame*, *envy*, *scorn*, *doom*, *sleep*, *misery*, *shadow*, *fate* and *plague.*

It was here where the Üngers were created, brought to dwell on this plane of being and to hunt down humans. Not including all the other servants of the dark he had convoked into being, over four hundred of them now roamed this world upon his command. Two, he knew, had been spiritually eviscerated. In the water of the black marbled font, he was shown their respective elimination by the separate actions of John Savage and Pall Warren under the warding of two Sentinel Trees. The priest's hate for these two humans and for all the ancient copper beeches was unrivaled by any other issue, except for his malevolence against the world itself.

His desire for their demise was uppermost in his mind. He had been working on conjuring up and creating another metaphysical weapon. He wanted something straightforward that had an acrid virulence to its sentience as well as an immediate seductive element that would be virtually impossible for a man to oppose in any way. His guides showed him a menu of sorts, from which he could select the most potent energies of wickedness that he could assemble together.

He was attracted to creatures called sirens, wendigos and zombies. Yet, they were not suitable for his purposes. Instead, he was permitted by the darknesses to create a hybrid demon based upon two creatures. One was called a *teyollocuani*, and the other a *souruita*. Both names translate as soul eaters.

He shortened the names into the word "Slake," which he thought was a clever combination, as it represented the need to quench, as well as fuel, another desire. The term also connoted the word snake. He pictured the Slake as an entity that was not only wraithlike but wreathlike, too. Its power of seduction, once engaged with a human, would twine itself onto a man's or a woman's body with the purpose of consuming one's energy and consciousness.

The Slake was a stunningly beautiful woman whose skin color was multihued. When the Slake was done feeding, the body of its victim turned to dust. The self that belonged to the human was used by the Slake to keep its form in the corporeal world. If the Slake could not obtain another victim, it had to return to the darkness from which it originated, while taking the consciousness of its victim with it as well.

Kosem Mungadai was in an ecstatic state. The trance he had entered placed him in an off–world location. He hovered, suspended in the air, above a massive waterfall. The power of the water roaring over the cliffs helped fuel his anger. He used it to bring forth two Slakes into being. One was assigned to the bowman and the other was sent to the young warrior.

CHAPTER NINE

Savage had spent the time since his meeting with Braucus Peredurus trying to keep occupied. He was waiting to hear back regarding the results of the Minister's investigation into the character and sympathies of Gregor Mordant.

Two or three times a day, he went to the Great Bay Tavern to eat and to see if Stephan Sayer was ready to meet with him, or to tell him the Minister wanted to arrange a time to get together with the archer. Sometimes he would just sit in the tavern and listen to the surrounding conversations, hoping to catch any word of what was happening in the city around him.

He started visiting the King's summer court in the mornings, when it fully convened, to hear the petitions being brought before the Crown with the hopeful expectation that he would hear about, or see, Gregor Mordant.

On the third day of not hearing from anyone, he suspected he was being followed.

Savage took counter surveillance measures to check on whether or not it was true that he was under some form of observation. He discovered not only that it was indeed being done, but it was being done discreetly and professionally.

He did not let on that he knew he was being watched. Thanks to his sense of irony, he was actually satisfied that someone was interested in him. Due to the competency of the people watching him, he knew it was from one of the King's more sophisticated intelligence networks.

Most likely, Gregor Mordant's people have taken an interest in me, he thought to himself.

The big man decided the best way to get to the Commander was not just to let Mordant find and follow the bowman, but to turn the tables on him by shadowing those following him.

By the fifth day of waiting to see the Minister, Savage understood the patterns, people and measures of observation being conducted against him. He also knew where the people watching him went after their surveillance on him was done. He even knew where they lived.

On the sixth and seventh days, he closely began to monitor the places where Mordant's men and women assigned to Savage went to report. Based on listening to the conversations he could hear, he narrowed down two locations where the probability of Mordant's appearing would most likely occur.

One was in the neighborhood within close vicinity to the Church of Equity that was at the inside edge of the northern defensive wall. This posed some problems of access because it was in a densely packed part of the city.

The other location was on the waterfront, due south of its counterpart, in one of the merchant guild's storage warehouses. While this place was opposite in character to the one in the city, it posed the equivalent problem of access because of its remoteness. Any approach to it would put him out in the open where he could be easily seen.

On the evening of the seventh day, he decided that he needed an interim strategy to put into play. He made the decision that he would kidnap one person from each location and interrogate him for what he knew. His goal was to take two people, one apiece on the eighth and ninth nights, whether or not he met with the Minister in the meantime.

Savage also sensed that he was being lured into a confrontation with Mordant. This realization, besides being instinctual, was practical.

After all, it would be something I would expect from someone of his professional caliber.

For some reason he did not choose to examine closely, this last thought further entertained his sense of irony as well.

The morning of the eighth day in which he had not been given any word or intimation of his upcoming meeting with the Minister of Affairs, the bowman resolved that he was going to visit the King's court. Instead of stopping in at the Great Bay Tavern, he bypassed it and proceeded to the seat of the summer government.

The King's court convened in a section of the palace and its fortress that was almost on the same level as that of his private quarters. The views of the city and Great Bay were stunning. Savage thought that the decision to build the court at such a beautiful overlook was a wise decision on the part of the original builders. Almost every inhabitant of the city had been there. Many would visit just to soak in the beauty of the architecture set amidst the natural scenic beauty surrounding it on all four sides.

The bowman arrived well before any business of the court was started. The place was literally deserted. To his surprise, however, one of the men who had been following him was in the hallway leading to the court itself. By chance, they approached one another. While Savage was entering the area, this other man was leaving. They walked by each other on opposite sides of the hall.

The bowman had to use all the discipline he could muster not to accost the man and take him into capture. Neither direct looks nor spoken words were exchanged between them.

Savage listened intently to the man's footsteps walking away from him. Satisfied that the man shadowing him had followed the course of the hallway to its exit point out of the building housing the King's court, the archer proceeded to the guarded entrance of the court itself.

One of the four guards posted at the great arabesque shaped doors nodded his head slightly in familiarity to Savage. Another opened one of the doors to allow him access inside.

Proceeding into the interior of the court, the bowman picked a place where he could clearly see the throne upon which the King sat to hear the petitions before him. Savage could also easily view the space before the throne where the petitioners stood to plead their cases before King Ranulf Ealhhere.

There were hand carved, stone benches along the wall where he stood. He sat down on one of them. Without realizing it, he fell asleep.

He awoke when he heard the first call of the court to order.

Looking around him, he saw that the courtroom had become densely crowded with Seascale citizens, visitors, onlookers and other members of the King's government, as well as a scattering of foreign dignitaries and envoys. Savage was quite interested in the court proceedings that were processed throughout the morning. He paid particular attention to what was happening throughout the court room. He noted and listened carefully to what he observed and heard in many of the subsidiary conversations and discussions occurring around him.

It was not until two hours after the sun reached its zenith in the sky above the court that the King decided to hold a recess. With much pomp and fanfare, he left the great court room. As he disappeared from view with his retainers following him, the big man caught a glimpse of Gregor Mordant among those trailing after the King.

Savage sauntered after them, quickening his pace when he reached the hallway they had gone down that led toward the center of the palace gardens.

Hearing them go out of the building and into the grounds of the fortress, he proceeded to the door through which they had exited. The big man went to the door and looked out at them. As they were descending on a stone path away from him, he could easily pick out Mordant walking alongside a cleric who was wearing an alabaster white robe.

The two were in an animated conversation. People walking nearby with them were listening and smiling at their conversation.

Savage could hear their voices, but they were too far away for him to distinguish what they were saying to one another.

While watching them walk further away, he saw the cleric put his hand on Mordant's right shoulder.

The cleric turned as though he could feel Savage watching him. The thaumaturge looked directly at the doorway in which the bowman had just been standing.

Savage did not see the priest's feral smile.

CHAPTER TEN

Although Braucus Peredurus did not admit being perturbed over Savage's misgivings regarding Gregor Mordant, the Minister was deeply affected by the bowman's doubts about the Commander. After meditating on this issue, Braucus admitted to himself that he had an instinctual distrust for Mordant as well. This apprehension had bothered him for a long time, but he could never admit it to himself consciously. Now that it was out in the open, he knew it was time for him to vet the man all over again as if he were a new recruit.

The trouble with this newly admitted information was that Gregor was not a freshly and newly minted member of the Minister's espionage team; Mordant was a senior player in it. Further, he was almost on a peer, or equal, level in seniority as Peredurus was on the King's staff. Any overt moves that the Minister might make to investigate the Commander would come to the other man's notice and attention, if not the King's as well.

Officially, the King's Minister of Affairs decided to stop, at least on the surface and to anyone watching him carefully, communicating with the bowman. On the outside, Braucus made it look as though he left the bowman out in the cold.

Peredurus wanted to even the playing field by seeming to cut the archer loose from his network.

Doing so, he considered, *will put a lot of talk out there about it. I will ask my people to pay attention to this chatter and see what turns up from it.*

However, the Minister could be a startlingly cautious man, and this level of discretion was shown in assigning some of his best people to follow Savage and put him under observation. Doing so would ease Braucus' concern about the bowman's wellbeing and also be a check on his loyalty to the Minister's cause. He did not want to be in the middle of a potential false play by anyone, even if it was by Savage himself, whom Peredurus greatly respected.

After meeting with Savage on the war galley, the Minister cautiously put out feelers on Mordant. He only relied on people he trusted the most and who had been in his service for decades. No one person knew the whole context of this subtle investigation. However, as the days, and then the week, passed since he had met with the bowman, Peredurus, bit by bit, uncovered disturbing evidence about Mordant.

The Commander's relationship with the apparently innocuous priest, Kosem Mungadai, became quite suspect. Nonetheless, the Minister believed that the time was not right to alert the King to this news. Also, the information he had gathered and compiled on the Commander, and the priest, was too fragile still. All he had to go on was his own "nose" for deceit as well as intelligence about these two men that was anecdotal and based on loose conjecture.

Patiently, circumspectly, and meticulously, Peredurus watched the moves made by Savage, Mordant and Mungadai. Countermeasures and contingency plans were prepared, put in place and readied on a proactive basis. He began to see a true and disturbing picture about the Commander and the priest. Braucus took great pains to protect his friend John Savage, but these measures would only be taken as end game scenarios. The bowman was on his own for now.

The small keg of Cabernet Sauvignon that was brought with great care from the southern tip of Umbria was never sent to John Savage.

CHAPTER ELEVEN

On the eighth night of not hearing from regular channels of communication in contacting the Minister, Savage captured a man from the city at the edge of the northern defensive wall. He had followed the archer for almost an hour and a half. The bowman had taken random routes throughout Seascale and even went out of the dung gate on the western side of the port city.

When Savage saw that the other man was too loathe in following him through this gate, the big man doubled back and turned the tables on his watcher by tracking him all the way to his headquarters near the Church of Equity.

One neighborhood away from arriving back to these city quarters, the bowman had anticipated his route and waylaid him in the darkest section of the street leading to his opponent's safe house. Savage had let the man pass by where the bowman had been standing in a recessed doorway. The archer quickly caught up to the man, wrapped one long arm around the other man's neck and choked him into unconsciousness.

He carried the man over his shoulder to a side lane that was almost completely enfolded in the dark by houses that leaned over towards one another from both sides of the narrow street. Savage had rented one of the houses here for the purpose of bringing this man to it for more extensive interrogation.

Taking a steady gait toward the middle house on the left side of this lane, he arrived quickly to it. The door was already unlocked. He let himself inside and put the man on a meat cutting table, which the bowman had borrowed from the nearby farmers' market. The board was purposefully left unclean. It stank of the gore and entrails of the butcher's daily work.

Savage lit several candles and prepared the space for the questioning of his prisoner. He closed and secured the shutters to the room's single window. He took one of the smaller rugs and hung it over the window to ensure that no errant light escaped to the outside.

A tarpaulin was already on the floor upon which the meat cutting table stood. A smaller table was placed at the side of the one where the man's body was set. It was near his head where he could see it when he regained consciousness, which Savage knew was imminent. On this smaller table was arrayed a set of tools, such as a variety of hammers, chisels, knives and grips.

The bowman secured his captive firmly to the table with several ropes that he had made ready beforehand for such a purpose. He left the man's head free.

Within minutes of tying the man to the table, his victim revived.

Savage let him regain complete consciousness. With a trace of solicitude, he brought a drink to the man's lips and held the cup so that the man was able to drink from it.

The captive drank the liquid greedily.

"So, Nigel," the bowman said with familiarity, "it appears that you have literally had the tables turned on you."

Nigel did not verbally respond to this comment. Instead, he signed with his head that he wanted more to drink.

Patiently, Savage propped Nigel's head up with one hand and let him drink his fill from the cup held to his mouth with the bowman's other hand.

Nigel nodded his head after he was through drinking from the cup. He closed his eyes briefly and opened them again.

Looking directly at the big man, he sincerely said, "Thanks for the murrey."

"My pleasure, Nigel."

"I prefer the black mulberries rather than blackberries," Nigel said referring to the ingredients in the hard cider from which he was drinking. He sighed deeply. "Despite my scruples, however, may I have another sip?"

Without saying anything, Savage readily obliged the man.

"Yes, indeed, Master Savage," Nigel said after he had taken another deep draught from the murrey, "the tables are not only turned, I am on one, thanks to you. But the phrase is from the game of shesh besh, or backgammon, not tables, literally."

The archer smiled gently, again remaining silent.

"We have been following you for a bit," Nigel stopped in the middle of his statement and licked his lips several times. "May I?" he asked indicating he wanted another drink of cider.

The cup was obligingly given to him as before. He took several more generous swallows from it.

Nigel's cheeks began to flush a slight red. He peered over at the other table laden with the tools and instruments Savage had placed on it. Nigel laughed when he realized what was on it.

Savage put the cup down from which Nigel had been quenching his thirst. The archer walked toward the door to the room, opened it and stepped out, closing the door behind him.

Eventually, Nigel started humming a tune he had known since his childhood. After several minutes of figuring out the words, he broke out aloud into the words of the song.

"Oh, the woe of the show
is the crow won't glow
as he flies over the snow
of my heart.

I have fallen apart;
love simply won't start,
and I have lost the art
of trying.

I have gone to the hill;
I have made out my will:
and, still, I spill out the
tears of lying.

Oh, the woe of the show
is the crow won't glow
as he flies over the snow
of my heart."

Nigel sang the song three more times.

He was humming it lustily when Savage reentered the room and returned to his captive's side.

Nigel stopped humming. His eyes were glazed. Sweat shone over his face. "I know wat ya've done to me, Sasauch," he said blearily.

He laughed, shook his head and said, "Sausage!" It seemed to Nigel that the laughter was coming deep from the bottom of his feet and coursing through him like fire being fanned by a strong wind.

He threw up all over himself in the middle of one violent burst of hilarity.

Nigel quickly realized he could not breathe. Vomit covered his face and prevented him from drawing fresh air into his lungs. He started to panic. He thrashed on the table as much as he could, but he was tied down too well for him to move around much at all.

He stared piteously at Savage, uttering, "Nnnnnnneehhhh. Nnnneehhheeen."

The big man took a cloth from the other table. He efficiently and gently wiped away Nigel's disgorge from the captive's face and mouth.

Tears leaked out from Nigel's eyes.

He took ragged gasps of breath.

Slowly, his breathing returned to normal.

He was flushed completely red.

"Wha didgeya do ta me, Sporridge? Didcha ya pizen me?"

Savage leaned over slightly so that Nigel could get a good view of his face. He nodded yes to Nigel.

"It will slowly get worse," he answered the suffering man before him. "Before you choke to death on your own puke, you'll feel as though you're on fire and that needles are being put in you throughout your body."

"Wha dewya want fromm me?"

"Don't you worry about that, Nigel; you'll soon tell me all that I want to know. And then more than even you think you know."

Nigel shook, cried and gritted his teeth until his lips started to bleed. He gasped several times, and then all the pain went suddenly away.

"What are you doing to me, John Savage!?" he shouted.

"Nothing compared to what you and your kind wants to do with me, Nigel."

"The pain's gone!"

"It's coming back, momentarily," assured the archer. "When it does, you'll think hell is heaven compared to what follows.

"You have an antidote, don't you?" Nigel half asked and partially stated.

"Of course, my good partner in stealth."

"Give it to me, and I swear on my mother's grave, I will tell you what I know. Just don't let me back out on the street. Take me somewheres else. Anywheres safe away from here."

"Nigel, I am more than happy to oblige you. And I will do so. Yet, if you fail me in your promise, the tools you see here on this table next to you will be used. Most proficiently."

Nigel swore on his mother's grave that he would tell whatever he knew.

110

Savage gave him the antidote from another cup in which it was mixed with claret.

It took a while for Nigel to settle down. Just as he started going into a major paroxysm, the remedy in the claret he had taken started to take effect and mitigated the poison.

Soon, Nigel's body stopped its shaking.

He kept thanking Savage for not carrying through poisoning him.

He told Savage everything that he knew. Information about Mordant's spy system, his contacts, ongoing projects, and his relationship to Kosem Mungadai were spilled out to the archer in a rush of relief.

"Gregor Mordant will be at the city safe house three nights from now," Nigel informed the bowman.

Savage patted Nigel on his right shoulder. "Good man, Nigel. Now I'm going to give you another drink. It will make you pass out, that's all. When you wake up, you'll be on board a ship headed south of here. Don't ever return to Seascale. Understood?"

"Yes," Nigel said. He understood perfectly.

The ninth night saw Savage heading to the other safe house on the waterfront.

He straightaway understood that there would be no meeting, for some time, with the Minister, especially after the information the bowman attained from interrogating Nigel the previous night. Braucus had cut their ties with one another.

This fact did not bother the archer adversely at all. On the contrary, it sent him a message that corroborated the information Savage had shared with him during their last meeting about Gregor Mordant and Kosem Mungadai. Being shut down like this had happened to Savage several other times in his career with the Minister. Each time it had happened was due to the fact that the Minister was working in a compromised atmosphere of security.

Just be patient, the big man counseled himself, *and it will wash itself out.* He had implicit trust in Peredurus and the Minister's abilities to set things straight.

As he had been thinking through his situation, he saw that someone had picked up his trail and was tailing him. He knew it was a man who shadowed him; Savage could tell by the sound of the man's tread and the manner in which he walked. The bowman closely estimated even his follower's weight and height.

He let himself be stalked until he came to the first dark stretch of road leading to the section of the bay where the warehouse he was walking towards was situated. The stretch of the road dipped into a gentle swale. It reeked of musky and gamey odors, and had a salt tang smell like the ocean had just retreated from being there only a moment ago.

He had been walking on the right side of the lane. Knowing this section of the street, he knew that there was a large, broken and brick lined culvert on the left side of the road. He quickly and silently went to it. Savage lowered himself on top of the drain just above the outlet. He jumped down on its far side in order to place himself into a better attack position.

He heard booted footsteps still coming toward him on the right side of the road, approaching to an almost even position from where he was hiding.

When the man following him stopped walking, he was slightly ahead of Savage's position. A period of silence ensued, but the archer could hear the man breathing. Several times, the stalker sniffed his nose and spat toward the culvert where the big man patiently waited for an opportune time to spring on his victim. The man grunted once, slightly, and started walking normally away toward the warehouse.

It was pitch dark.

Savage sensed a trap was being prepared for him. With that thought in mind he unslung his bow and strung it.

He let the other man get toward the top of the swale where he could see him outlined in the night against the lights from the warehouses and the Great Bay itself.

Where he stood, he could feel gravel under his feet. The murmur of water flowed and gurgled quietly up to and around his knees.

Placing the shaft of the arrow on the bow's arrow rest, he quickly aligned the slot in the nock with the string. The arrow was a flare that he had specially made during the day. He had three of them in a full quiver that he carried over his right shoulder.

Holding the bow and nocked arrow in his left hand, he reached down underneath him and grabbed two handfuls of stones with his other hand.

Savage stood up to his full length.

There was no wind.

The stench of the harbor flooded his senses.

He saw that the man ahead had stopped and was waiting where he stood.

Knowing the road's contour, condition and course by memory, the archer threw the stones in several different arcs ahead of him to the right side of the lane. He was attempting to make it sound as though he had scuffed up and kicked rocks aside in an attempt to get off the road.

He heard several men rise up on both sides of the road in the vicinity where he had thrown the gravel. He lit the arrow inside the opening of the culvert where its light could not be seen by the men already on the road ahead. Once the arrow was lit, he stepped outside the culvert and leaned into the bow itself, aimed high overhead and released it.

The arrow flew in a huge curving trajectory over the swale.

Four men looked up at it in absolute surprise. Shock came to them next and suddenly.

Savage let loose three arrows, successively in a row, within seconds of each other.

One man was hit in the head, the arrow entering him just before the top of his right ear where his middle temporal artery and vein were located. Punching through the temporal bone as though it were freshly made cake, it went into the medulla oblongata, raised havoc there because of the arrowheads he was using in this instance and stuck through the other side of his head.

The man was dead before he was aware of what happened to him.

The second arrow caught another man in the chest where his heart was located. It went through the ribs at the third intercostal space, completely destroying the left side of the heart where the ventricle and auricular esquerras were placed. The arrow drilled through the rest of the body, hitting and bouncing off the left thigh of the fourth man without doing any damage except psychological bewilderment.

Smashing into the right side of the third man's waist with explosive force, the last arrow Savage fired went through both kidneys of its intended victim. It also went through the body, continuing into the dark off the far side of the road.

The archer, immediately after releasing the third arrow, set himself in motion and charged the group of men, now left to one man standing alone in wonderment over what had transpired.

As the bowman ran by him, Savage struck him on the top of the head with a small sledge hammer that he had purchased the day before from a blacksmith. Grunting heavily, the fourth man crumpled to the ground.

Running toward the man at the top of the swale, and before the flare extinguished itself, the archer could see horror written on his expression. The remaining man turned and ran over the top of the rise in the road.

For every three steps the other man took, Savage made up for it with one of his own. Reaching the top of the rise in turn, the bowman saw that the other man was less than fifty feet away. Savage was slightly surprised that this individual had not gotten off the road and instead had just remained on it.

Within ten feet of him, he threw the sledge hammer at the back of the running man's head. The hammer happened to land face first on the center of the other man's parietal bone.

Stunned, the other man stopped running and dropped to his knees.

Savage ran up to him. When he turned and faced the man, he heard him exclaim, "All right, Savage, you have me. Just don't murder me. The demonstration in killing you just gave is enough for me."

The bowman, hardly out of breath, said, "Stand up, Giles, and walk ahead of me."

Complying with his command silently, Giles stood up and did as he was told.

Walking slowly ahead of the bowman, and rubbing the back of the top of his head, Giles complained, "In the name of the Priest Kosem Mungadai, what the hell are you going to do with me? Damn it, Savage, I'm bleeding like a stuck pig!"

The archer just pushed the man in the middle of the back with his bow.

When they reached the Great Bay, Savage told Giles to walk along it in the opposite direction of the warehouse.

A quarter of a mile later, the bowman prodded Giles into an empty shed next to a grindery. Inside the shed, scattered loosely on the floor, was a large assortment of tools that Savage had borrowed from the shop next door to the shed. Glistening from being honed to a razor's edge were, for example, knives, drills, punches, awls, chisels, axes, dirks, daggers, poniards, and swords.

Giles' eyes went wide when he recognized what was in front of him laid out on the floor.

Savage watched the other man's eyes narrow in thought.

The bowman, using the index finger of his right hand, stabbed Giles in the solar plexus. "Don't even entertain the notion of picking anything you see on the floor up in your hand. Right now, you're less than a blink of an eye from not being able to walk for the rest of your life."

Hearing this warning, Giles moved over to an empty spot against the far wall. He sat down heavily on his rump. He sighed and asked wearily, "What do you want to know, Savage?"

"Everything," the archer told him.

CHAPTER TWELVE

Giles' fate at the hands of the archer was a merciful one. Savage brought Giles to an empty apartment in the middle of the city. The big man made sure that the other man was rendered unconscious in a safe manner.

The second man Savage accosted now shared the same fate as the first one. While Nigel had been shipped south, Giles was sent west. Both men had delivered the same information under their separate interrogations.

The validation in the two stories given the bowman made him believe, somewhat confidently, that Mordant would be at the city safe house on the eleventh evening that Savage would be out of contact with Braucus Peredurus.

After seeing that Giles was safely sent on his way, he returned to the location where Mordant's men had planned to attack him. No one had been there; or, if they had, they had not disturbed any of the bodies of the men still lying on the roadside.

The bowman was only able to retrieve one of the three arrows he had used. The first one could not easily be taken out of the skull of his first victim. Instead of trying to remove it, he snapped off the shaft before the fletching and put it temporarily in his quiver. The second one he picked up off the street. He did not bother looking for the third one, or for the fourth arrow with the flare. Savage did not have the time to go searching for them in the dark, but he was not worried about these two arrows.

By the time anyone finds them, if they find them, it will be too late to do anything about it.

He dumped the four bodies in the culvert in which he had stood earlier in the night.

He expected that they would be searched for and found, which is what he hoped would occur. He smiled to himself at that thought.

After he finished this task, he returned to the inn where he was staying. Savage retired for the evening almost as soon as he got into his room. He slept the rest of the night contentedly and soundly on the floor alongside the bed.

No one disturbed him.

The bowman arose the next morning before dawn. He washed himself, got dressed in fresh clothes and went downstairs to the common room where he sat in a comfortable chair. As the room he was in faced east, he watched the sunrise. While doing so, a plan formed in his mind for his next moves against Mordant.

He planned on confronting the Commander in a showdown on the night Gregor was supposed to be in the city safe house. To make sure the plan had teeth in it, Savage intended on calling in help from his own people within his established networks. He thought he could put together sixty men, including about a dozen women who were formidable fighters in their own right, in the time allotted him to get Mordant.

Ideally, he wanted to capture him, but he did not think the chances of doing so favored this option. The Commander was too disciplined for such an incident to happen. Mordant would find some way, even suicide, to avoid being apprehended alive. Besides that, Gregor was in league with the priest, which made for another layer of difficulty in getting to him.

Savage spent the tenth day and night, as well as the early part of the eleventh morning, getting his forces together. He made contingency arrangements in case things went wrong or unfolded in different ways. The bowman basically prepared a battle plan for an armed, violent encounter with Mordant and the Commander's fellow combatants.

Within the city itself, he positioned his people in main and reserve forces with fallback positions. They were placed halfway between Mordant's safe house and the city center. On foot outriders, or urban pickets, were positioned on both sides in order to give the main force notice that an attack was imminent, or in the process of happening. They also were in place to help provide information as to the manner, method and numbers of those coming against them.

For appearance's sake, and to keep his opponents off balance, he wanted them to think that he was operating alone. After all, the Minister had severed ties with Savage. The bowman was vulnerable to a strike against him as he was reduced to being a majority of one against the full complement and combined might of Commander Mordant and his allies, as well as against those of the Church of Equity.

At noon on the eleventh day, the big man went to the Great Bay Tavern. He walked past the front entrance and went up the lane to the chestnut vendor. He purchased a small bag of them and retraced his way back to the tavern. He looked up at the tavern's sign when he reached its main entrance. It was not in motion. There was no wind coming off the bay, but it looked as though a rainstorm was in the offing later on during the day or early evening. Storm clouds were amassing in the western sky. He detected lightning flashing distantly in them.

Savage entered the building and walked over to the table at which he had become accustomed to sitting. There was a party of boisterous people already sitting there eating their noontime meal and drinking copious amounts of ale. Servers were constantly plying back and forth between them and the kitchen bearing plates of food and pitchers of newly poured ale to refresh their quickly drained cups.

He noticed that a small table for two people was vacant next to the right side of the kitchen door. He wended his way to this table. Reaching it without anyone else preceding him to the spot, the big man sat down in the chair that was further from the door into the kitchen. He placed a small gold coin face down in the bottom of the bag of chestnuts and waited to be served. He put the bag of chestnuts on the table before him.

He waited for the shadow of the sun inside the nearest tavern window to move the width of his little finger.

The tavern was full of people. No one served him.

An older woman bearing a half–loaded tray of empty cups and wooden plateware started to approach the door next to the other side of his small table. Savage stood up holding the bag of chestnuts in his left hand.

"'Scuse me, Miss," he said to her, "I know Billy in the buttery has a sweet tooth for chestnuts. Will ya give this to em fer me?"

The woman looked at him with a somewhat jaundiced eye.

"Here, make sure ya do. I kinda promised his ma I'd look after em."

The bowman placed the bag on her serving tray, which she had never taken off her shoulder. He shrugged his shoulders as if to ask, *What can you do in this world?*

He dug into his pockets and placed two small silver coins on the tray.

Her jaundiced look disappeared and she gave a hesitant smile.

Savage left the tavern room and sauntered back out onto the street.

He walked back to the inn and went to his room. He took the two pillows from the bed and put them on the floor even with the headboard. He put two blankets from the bed also on the floor and laid down on them.

Just before he went to sleep, he smiled. The signal had been given to Sayer, and through him to Peredurus, that the bowman was on the move. The hour of battle was approaching. Quickly falling asleep, Savage did not hear the thunder booming and rolling off into the distance. The wind picked up outside his window. Within the confines of its wooden frame, it spluttered out a staccato rhythm in accompaniment to his deep breathing.

The sound of the wind shrieking and whistling past the room where he slept left him undisturbed. The fury of the rain free falling from the sky and smashing against the building and panes of glass in the window left his sleep untroubled. Neither the flashes of lightning searing across the window nor the thunder practically roaring in his ear drums caused him to awake.

The sound of someone in a pair of boots treading lightly in the hallway outside his door, however, seemed as a signal, an alarm, for his eyes, and his awareness, to snap open.

There was no light in the room where he rested on the floor. This lack of illumination gave him a slight advantage because, when he looked underneath the door, he could clearly see beyond it. The newly alighted oil lamps, each positioned on two tables in the hallway, clearly lit up the corridor floor.

He watched intently as a pair of dirty brown leather boots stepped up to his door and were placed parallel to one another. Pointing off from the other in a twenty–degree angle, he saw that the man had brought himself to attention before the door.

Savage soundlessly stood up and walked silently over to the closed door. He approached it from the opposite side of its handle.

A soft rapping started in a series of four distinct knocks: one tap, quickly followed by three, and concluded with a single beat repeated once.

In the dark of the room, the archer smiled to himself. *It seems it's time for the chess pieces to be placed in motion.*

The bowman let the man outside his door knock twice more in the same fashion as executed with the first series of taps.

"Okay, Red, the door's unlocked," he said in a low toned voice.

Red came through the door cautiously and slowly, making sure that his hands were in clear sight of the big man behind it.

Upon seeing the man silhouetted in the entryway of the door, Savage moved into the room where his own dark form could be seen by Red.

"Have a seat on the bed and tell me what you know," he instructed the other man.

Red followed the directions given him. Sitting on the edge of the foot of the bed he informed Savage, "Everything's set in place and ready to go, John. The bad weather is our ally this night."

"Thank you," responded Savage, who went toward the window. "I appreciate what you and everyone else are doing."

"Mordant has put together a large collection of men against you," informed Red. "He knows you're after him. We think he's placed well over two hundred men throughout the city to trap you. They are concentrated, as you know, in three main places—the city safe house, the waterfront warehouse and the middle of the city."

"I would expect that he has taken such measures," remarked Savage. "He's a craven at his core. His sense of self-preservation comes first above everything else."

"He will be hard to catch then, John," replied Red.

Savage agreed with Red's statement. He nodded his head at the man. "We'll make it possible for him to show where he is burrowed in his den. When we put everything in motion, it will be interesting to see which way the fox will turn."

The archer closed to an arm's length away from the window and peered out from its left side casement into the gloomy and stormy weather.

Just for a while, the two men indulged themselves in the luxury of listening to the sounds of the gale outside the inn where Savage had been staying.

Fully armed, Savage arrived at Mordant's city safe house. He carried with him two loaded quivers, a brace of throwing knives, and two anelaces.

The anelace was a preferred weapon for the archer. Some fighters thought of it as a kind of short, two–sided sword, but Savage liked to think of it as a long dagger. In his hands, the anelaces indeed looked like smaller bladed arms. He used them in a similar fashion as those carrying a sword and parrying dagger would in a paired, hand–to–hand combat method.

He took up a position within sight of the main entrance of the safe house, and one that was in the shadows of the arched doorways out of the light of the street lanterns. He watched those entering and leaving the building. Carefully assaying the quality of their movements, he saw that everything appeared normal.

He did not believe, though, that the people he was observing were following their regular routines. The information he had obtained, the knowledge he had acquired and his accrued skill and experience in such matters, sent warning signals to his first tentative conclusions about what he was seeing.

Taking advantage of the appalling weather, as well as a lull in those going in and out of the safe house, Savage gained entrance into the building by going through a first–floor window he managed to open somewhat silently. What noise he did make was covered up by the storm raging down on him and the rest of the city.

The occupants of the safe house, being tipped off by their own lookouts about Savage's whereabouts, left it through the first–floor back doors, located at either end of the building.

The archer began a basement to attic search of the place. He was not looking only for Mordant, or for any other individuals, he wanted to see the place and absorb what was left in it for him to observe.

Moving from room to room in an efficient manner, he quickly reached the third floor. It was at this point he concluded he had been left alone in the building. He rolled up a twelve–foot corridor rug, and going all the way up the fourth–floor stairs, he threw it fifteen feet further into the hallway where it landed and partially unrolled against the other side of the wall. The hard flung carpet also struck a table from which a pitcher fell and shattered in pieces on the floor.

As the ceramic piece was being broken, Savage was back near the side of a window in one of the unlocked rooms on the third floor. Positioned there, with the window partially open, he heard a door on the first floor of the safe house slam shut. He heard someone running desperately away down the street away from him.

Kosem Mungadai had let a Slake loose into the house.

CHAPTER THIRTEEN

Captain Eumero was playing a stalling action with Pall and Merek. They knew what he was doing in this regard. He knew that they were aware of his delaying tactics. Everyone knew what the other was doing, and they each understood it was a deadly game.

The Captain did not bring them directly downriver to Seascale. Rather, he made several unaccounted stops along the Forgotten River. What ordinarily took five to seven hours of time to reach the port city from Gullswater was taking him the full day. He stopped for fresh water from a spring located up one of the river's tributaries. Even though they had enough fresh water aboard, and could have gotten more easily from the river itself, Eumero made the excuse that he was quite partial to this spring water.

"It's the best I've ever tasted," he said as a poor excuse for stopping.

What momentum had been established moving downstream with the current was completely wrecked by the time he and some of his men went to get five, twenty-five gallon barrels of water from this "eagerly" sought elixir.

Other stops were made to provision five different caches that Eumero felt were important to keep freshly stocked.

"You never know when you need to use them," he said lamely, knowing full well that in offering such a reason, it was still a dissatisfactory rationale to give. The supposed purpose of the trip was to deliver Pall and Merek safely and on a timely basis to the city. This goal, obviously more and more as the day went by, became fully unattainable.

In two places where they stopped, Pall thought the Captain and his men were going to try to overwhelm Merek and him. Both times before violence almost broke out among them, Eumero would break out in laughter and talk about peace among friends.

His talking to them became increasingly fraught with tension. It got to the point when no more conversations occurred between them.

Pall and Merek were careful not to get in a tight spot with any of the crew, or even to turn their backs on any one of them.

As the light of day waned, it began to rain.

It was a bona fide downpour by the time *La Signora Maria* made one more final stop beside another longboat anchored out of the lanes of maritime traffic in the Great Bay.

Looking at the severity of the storm and reacting to the accompanying sound of rolling thunder booming around him, Merek thought, *This cursed weather is fit for the falseness of everyone put together on this foul vessel.*

131

Lightning lit up everything around them. It intertwined itself in complex patterns throughout the low scudding cumulous clouds overhead. The smell of its electrical discharges singed the air in a sharp, acrid odor.

Storm lanterns had been lit and were set up abaft and upon the fore of both longboats, as well as on their midships railing.

The young men did not know the purpose of this last stop, but they knew it did not bode well for them. A skiff manned by several men was deployed from the other boat and headed ashore before *The Lady Mary* again got underway.

It was nighttime and still raining heavily as they were brought to what seemed like an abandoned wharf. It was in a major state of disrepair. Although, when the longboat docked at its berth, fresh ropes from the pier side were used to tie off the ship.

The water cascading down upon them was frozen in appearance from the discharge of lightning.

Merek, at first shocked by the power of the lightning flashes, nevertheless was able to notice that the bollards to which the longboat was secured were also freshly placed. The low tide ladders to climb up to the pier itself were made of new sawn lumber.

Pall put himself into an enhanced state of awareness and readiness for any sudden moves against the two of them.

Eumero and his second in command, each holding a storm lantern, got off the ship with Pall and Merek.

Half a dozen men from the nearby warehouse came out to the wharf to meet the new arrivals. They were also carrying several storm lanterns.

"You lads are welcome to come in and dry yourselves off inside," offered Eumero.

"No, thank you, Captain," replied Merek.

"At least take these two lights with you. It's a cold, brisk night that sees you ill prepared for such foul weather."

"Grazi, Captain Eumero," replied Merek. As he and Pall each took a proffered lamp, Merek added, "My associate and I thank you for your kindness in taking us here safely."

"Think nothing of it. Avere una serata sicura, amico!" Eumero said with what Merek thought looked like a shark's grin on the captain's face.

"And you, Capitano, have a safe evening as well!" responded Merek.

The six men who had come out to greet Eumero quietly positioned themselves in a half circle around the four of them.

Eumero clapped Merek on his left shoulder. Both the Captain and his second turned away from them and headed toward the shelter of the warehouse. The two senior officers of *La Signora Maria* filed between the other six from the warehouse.

Pall remained stock still waiting for a signal to be made to attack him.

None came. No attack was made.

The six men—one in particular shrugged his shoulders and smiled toothlessly at Pall—turned around and followed the Captain into the ramshackle building he had just entered.

A brilliant electric discharge of light went off over the warehouse. Almost immediately following its display of searing white light, a crack of thunder shook everything around them. It rumbled off into a crumbling stutter.

It was at that point that another boat, a coble in fact, virtually collided into the pier in back of Captain Eumero's longboat. In his haste to get out of the power of the storm, the captain of this boat misjudged the distance left to him in order to properly berth the high–bowed craft.

The sound of the coble crashing into the dock, and the shouts of the men on board it, brought the full complement of men out of the warehouse and back into the storm to see what all of the pandemonium was about on their wharf.

Pall and Merek joined them to help those on board the coble tie it up against the pier in a storm rigging fashion. They also had to bring the coble away from the longboat because it was too close to it for either boat to be safe from further damage.

Eumero sent his second in command to help the crew remaining on board *La Signora Maria* move the longboat further away from the coble.

Eumero went over to the other boat to help aid the captain there. While the coble's captain was immersed in taking care of onboard concerns, Eumero oversaw those on the docks. Several men had fallen overboard when the coble had smashed into the pier. They had to be fished out of the bay's turbulent waters. This procedure was not an easy one because the men participating in the rescue attempts had to be careful and take account of a large, violently moving boat that was riding up and down against the wharf.

Ladders were disintegrating, rope lines were being snarled and snapped, and broken parts of the newly arrived craft were dropping off of it in a rain of its own making.

It got to the point that men holding the storm lanterns played as important a part as those helping secure the coble and those trying to get men out of the water.

It took well over an hour for matters to sort themselves out.

When the two boats were secured and everyone was safe, Eumero and the captain of the coble brought everyone back into the warehouse.

A keg of rum was opened and its contents shared with all present.

Eumero expressed surprise and concern that Merek and Pall were not present. A search was organized to find them, but failed in its end result. The young men were gone.

Just as the plight of the two boats, and the men overboard, was being resolved by the attempts of the three groups of men, Pall walked over to Merek and signed to him that it was time to leave the pier. The young warrior thought that it was an excellent time to disappear. They had just rescued an older man from the water at the stern of the coble boat.

The two young men brought the man to the warehouse and saw to him being wrapped in a blanket and set before a fire in the main room of the warehouse.

Merek nodded in agreement with Pall's sentiment to leave at an opportune moment as the one that now made itself available to them.

In the confusion and mayhem of the collision, and with the covering of the fierce weather confronting everyone present, the two young men walked away from it all at a normal pace. They promptly reached the edge of darkness away from the light of the storm lanterns. Even before they approached the end of the pier, they were covered and concealed in the penumbra, and then absolute obscurity, of the night.

Merek led Pall into the city. He seemed intimately familiar with his urban surroundings. He led Pall through the night's storm and gloom, passing under the flickering light of oil lanterns and candles in the windows of houses, and lightning snapping overhead. Through back alleys, deserted streets and the shadows of buildings thrown onto main thoroughfares from torches still burning and yet thickly smoking from the rain's incessant inundation, Merek headed toward a place safe from the prying eyes of Mordant's men.

He went to his childhood home in the east end of Seascale.

Pall did not realize that they had reached the end of their night's journey as he found himself in the wealthiest part of the city. Well–spaced stone mansions, set sideways to one another, stretched up and down both sides of one of the widest streets they had traversed. Glazed windows, ranging from ornately to simply designed stained glass in them, and massively constructed chimneys ensconced within slate tiled roofs, all helped to create an impression of luxury, wealth, respectability and security.

Merek stopped at a mansion that was bracketed on either side by town houses enfolded completely over by scaffolding. Contemporary and more imposing buildings were rising from their former estates.

Instead of walking up to an impressive looking, hand carved wooden door, he followed the stone pathway to the right of it. It led past the main house to one of the caretakers' houses in the back. Merek walked in to the kitchen area, urging the still gawking Pall to do likewise.

"Whose place is this?" Pall asked.

"You mean the place we're in?" Merek countered.

"No, Yes," the young warrior said with bewilderment.

Merek smiled kindly. "The main house belongs to my parents. The house we're in right now is untenanted. It's still fully stocked and ready for someone to move in. But my parents never saw the need for another caretaker and his family to help manage the grounds on this smaller estate of theirs in the city."

Pall still wore a disconcerted expression.

"We have a much larger estate, an extensive manor, really, in the country. It's a little over a day's journey from here by wagon. That's where our second caretaker is needed, and then several more."

Pall made a soundless "oh" expression on his face.

Merek laughed. "Look, we're here to get a change of clothes and something to eat. I need some weapons from our armory. Maybe you can choose a weapon or two that might strike your fancy also," he offered.

Pall nodded at this series of suggestions.

Merek ignored him. He went into the larder and brought out cheese, ale, grapes, dried meat and freshly made bread. He served both of them the food and beverage.

Pall shook his head in amazement.

"Well, get out of your state of shock," Merek admonished the warrior. "I need your full attention."

"Thank you, Merek, truly," Pall managed to say.

"When we're finished here, we're going back to that warehouse."

"Okay," Pall responded.

"I just know Mordant will be there. Asutuo and Eumero will have tipped him off that we are here. He'll come looking for us."

"Okay," Pall again stated.

Merek, finishing the food before him, looked worriedly at Pall. He gathered up the plates, cups, and extra food in his hands and arms and brought them to a side table. He quickly wiped the plates and cups off, put all the implements and food back in place and made sure that everything else was left just as clean as when they first entered the stone cottage.

He then almost had to lead Pall by the elbow to get him to follow him upstairs. Here, Merek changed his clothes. Pall declined to change his, but he did take the light wool cloak Merek offered him. It was a beautifully made one. Dyer's woad had been professionally applied to color the cloth a deep, dark blue.

Leaving the cottage, they went to the armory, which was a one story, circular, brick built building. It was located towards the back wall of the estate. He retrieved a key from underneath a pile of wooden shutters stacked on top of ash logs that formed the base of the pile.

Upon entering the building, he lit several oil lamps. When the room was flooded with light, Pall saw one of the most complete, civilian collection of weapons he had ever had the privilege to observe.

"Quickly, Pall, go through the place and pick out what you would like to have," he urged.

Pall looked at what was arrayed around him. He quickly adjusted to appraising everything in the arsenal. He took a couple of daggers. He became fascinated with a quarterstaff weighted with round metal ferules on both ends.

Merek saw the desire to have it on Pall's face and urged him to take it, which the young warrior did with alacrity. He affixed it to a specially made sling that enabled him to place it over his back without hindering the drawing and use of his falchion sword.

They doused the lamps. Merek locked the door and put the key to it back where he found it.

The weather still being the same, they retraced their steps to the waterfront warehouse where they first landed in the port city. Lightning helped illuminate what they were trying to see. The two men carefully watched the place for signs of human activity. No one seemed to be present. They entered the building and began a full investigation of the place.

They reached the far end of the warehouse without delay. It was here when they heard a door slam shut at the front end of the building where they had entered it. A set of footsteps could be heard faintly running farther down the wharf away from the building.

Pall and Merek looked at one another.

"This is very much familiar to me, Merek," Pall stated bluntly.

"Yes, it is," Merek answered in kind.

"This is eerily just like the night we had at the farmstead with the Ünger."

Merek shut his eyes briefly and nodded grimly.

Mordant, having left the Church of Equity, had arrived here on the waterfront. The Commander had let a Slake loose into the warehouse.

CHAPTER FOURTEEN

The bowman grimaced. Had he even a partial shot at the man fleeing away from the safe house, Savage would have taken it. But it was not to be this time.

He made a hurried assessment of the remainder of the third floor and descended back down to the second. As the archer walked down the wooden stairs to the second floor, he received a distinct impression that someone, or something, else was in the building with him. The oil lamps had been left burning, despite the fact that the people who formerly were inside the safe house had gone. Perchance, it was a sequence of moving shadows that engaged his instincts. Conceivably, it might have been a slight creaking noise that did not belong to the normal sounds of a building shifting on its own base, or the sounds of it responding to the wildness of the weather outside beating against it.

Faster than the eye could move, Savage had the pair of anelaces removed from their sheaths and in his hands as he completed his descent down to the second floor.

Hypersensitive to the air in the rooms and hallway through which he was moving, the big man started to feel unnaturally closed in.

I am suffocating, he said to himself.

Appraising his feelings and emotions in concert with his rational understanding, he decided that he was not taking any further chances on being trapped, or falsely engaged in a minor distraction. His goal was to take Mordant, not fight one, or likely more of his flunkies.

Opening a window at the far end of the north side of the safe house, he climbed out of it, clambering down a nearby drain pipe that extended to the ground.

Once on the street and across from the building, he looked up at the window out of which he had just climbed. He saw the lineation of a woman standing in the middle of its frame.

Savage shuddered. He was relieved to be away from inside the safe house.

After the silhouette of the woman moved away from where she had stood, the bowman made the immediate decision to go to Mordant's other safe house on the waterfront.

Lightning broke open the dark around him. Not seeing anyone, the archer quickly moved towards his new objective.

Thunder grumbled off in the distance, sounding like a giant disgruntled with the world he was viewing.

The anelaces were still in Savage's hands.

After the bowman had raced by him at the end of the street where the safe house was situated, a man's shape detached itself from underneath the overhang of an apothecary shop. The thaumaturge wore a slight smile on his face. Mungadai had seen the bowman climb out of the window to escape being caught in the clutches of the creature he had created. He could not help but admire Savage's abilities in evading the Slake.

Reaching the corner of the street he had been on, the priest walked down an intersecting one where he joined a group of his men.

Oblivious to the weather, he gave instructions to his captains on deploying the forces he had positioned around the safe house since it had been first under Savage's observation that evening. Except for a standing contingent of fifty men, he sent the rest of them after the archer.

To palliate the deadly, sensual sensibilities of the creature he had sent into the city safe house after the bowman, Mungadai sent two of his own men, whom he least favored, into it to their doom.

Sensing a stratagem was being used against them, Merek led Pall out of the warehouse through one of its back doors. They successfully got away from the building and back out on another road that led along the waterfront. Merek leaned over towards Pall as they were walking along the long curving road that followed the contour of the bay back to the city.

Almost having to shout aloud his words, he told Pall that the best thing they could do to get a hold of Mordant was to head towards the Commander's safe house in the city.

As a way of confirming Merek's words, Pall clapped his comrade's right shoulder twice.

Merek decided that they would take the long way around and approach the center of the city from another direction than would be expected of them. They could then take an alternate, but parallel, set of roads to the safe house from that point.

In the meantime, Mordant had waited outside the warehouse for the Slake to do its business inside. He waited for what he believed was an appropriate amount of time for the creature to accomplish its task. However, after standing at the end of the wharf in the rain longer than he expected, he became suspicious that something had run afoul.

Everything was too quiet for his comfort.

First, he sent one of his men to investigate, warning the man to be circumspect in his checking to see what was happening inside the building. The man never came back out of the warehouse.

145

Mordant sent another man inside and had his men surround the building.

Again, all was quiet inside; yet, no one came back outside.

Taking a gamble at making a decision on what to do strategically, Gregor thought, *If the lightning doesn't flash over the next several minutes, I'll head everyone back to the city safe house.*

Thunder muttered away in the distance.

The rain came down harder than ever before.

Mordant started thinking about a similar evening when he and Error had gotten drunk in the warehouse when they first met there fifteen long years ago. Error had just been accepted as a Marauder. He had accidentally burned the palm of his hand grabbing a log that had fallen from the fire that they had started after they began to get very inebriated. Gregor, mistakenly grabbing the same log Error had touched, ended up burning himself, too.

The Commander could still hear Error's raucous laughter, ringing off the walls of the warehouse, at the Commander's expense.

The master spy gave a start. He realized he had drifted off and lost track of the time. He shook the memory of Error away from himself. Putting his fingers to his lips, he gave a sharp, short whistle.

It was his signal for his men to deploy back to the city safe house.

CHAPTER FIFTEEN

Peredurus was in a decidedly sullen and fractious mood. He kept staring at the keg of Cabernet Sauvignon that he had left in his office where he had, especially of late, been spending an inordinate amount of time trying to get all of his work done.

He refused to tap open the keg. He even had put a tag with Savage's name listed on it to help reserve it for his longtime friend and ally. *After all, it was promised to John*, he said to himself. *When all of this situation sorts itself out, I'll be sure that he gets it for his own enjoyment.*

The Minister had been carefully monitoring Savage and knew that the bowman was putting together his own force of over seventy people. Peredurus expected no less of the big man.

Braucus had received the last bag of chestnuts with the gold coin in the bottom of it. The image of the late King Warin Ealhhere was face down, which was a signal that Savage had not wanted to, or could not, meet with the Minister. It also meant that the archer was on perilous duty and could not do so. Stephan Sayer had brought the bag to Peredurus, along with the message about Savage's last attempt to be in formal communication with the Minister.

Peredurus smiled at the story of John tipping the woman server, who happened to be Stephan's wife

Glenda, with two silver coins. He recalled what Sayer had reported the big man said to her and the manner in which it was said.

Thunder sounded in the distance outside his window, which overlooked one of the most beautiful views of the castle grounds, Seascale and the Great Bay. He had walked over to it to look out at the view. A scattering of large, fat droplets of rain fell on the back of his hands as he leaned upon the open window sill. The breeze picked up. He could smell the rain coming his way.

A squall is dumping a lot of rain over the mouth of the bay, he silently mused.

It was getting dark outside, and he was still in his office where he had been since dawn this morning. He started the day receiving corroborating truth from several reliable and trustworthy sources about Kosem Mungadai's history. From that point on, and over the next six hours, other reports came in that indicted the priest even further.

What the Minister found particularly concerning were the plans, including the foreign and domestic relationships the priest had developed, that were all pointing towards his preparations for war against the northern realms. West Fündländ and the Western Isles were the primary targets of invasion and revolution.

Above and beyond all of this information given to him about the thaumaturge was something that disturbed him even more about the priest's very identity. No one, at least to this point in time, could definitively state from where the man originated.

It's as though he doesn't belong here, he brooded.

Braucus decided to take this information to the King. He notified the King's secretary that he was dropping by the inner court right after the King had finished his lunch, and before His Highness was scheduled to go back to the outer court to arbitrate petitions before the Crown for that afternoon.

A foul up in relaying this information occurred. King Ealhhere understood that his Minister of Affairs wanted to see him after the King was done rendering his decisions for the day.

Peredurus finally was able to see him late in the afternoon. When he was admitted into the King's Chambers in the inner court, Ranulf Ealhhere was exhausted from his day's work. He was also petulant about making decisions that had gone against his better judgment, but were instead made for political rather than for personal reasons.

This irritation was brought into the meeting he had with his Minister. It overrode everything else. Thus, when Braucus brought his vetted information about the priest and Mordant to the King's attention, it was rejected out of hand by Ealhhere.

The King's Minister left the meeting now equally in as foul a mood as his Lord.

Walking away from the chamber in the corridor leading to the outer court, Peredurus said softly aloud to himself, "At least he granted me permission to assemble a greater security force together."

Returning to his office, he spent the remaining daylight hours left to him integrating the seventy–five men the King had granted him into the hundred twenty–five men he already had assembled together. He was frustrated and disappointed that he only had been able to amass a final force of two hundred men. His feelings aside, Braucus made the determination to position the men into two key points.

As he was aware of Gregor Mordant's activity and the force of about fifty–five men he was gathering, he also knew where it was being deployed in the city and on the waterfront. The Minister was cognizant of the fact that Mordant ordered several captains and their respective longboats to be positioned on the bay in three places. He speculated that these boats and their crews were to be used either as a conveyance of more men and matérial and/or as a means of escape from the city.

Braucus had been fully apprised by his observers about Mungadai putting together at least two hundred twenty–five of his followers, as well as a scattering of cut throats, murderers and wanted criminals. He was alert to the priest placing this force in the center of the city. The fact, in and of itself, that Mungadai was at the nerve center of this treachery against the Realm was proof enough for the Minister of the priest's guilt and culpability in actively plotting revolution against the Crown and threatening the peace and security of the Kingdom.

Based upon his latest information and the estimates of the forces at play, Peredurus put his own two forces at the northern and southern ends of the city. He placed observers and their complementary runners so that they were able to monitor all four groups being **arrayed against one another. Two of the largest streets in Seascale, Dolphin and Guild,** happened to converge in the center of the port city. He planned on using these roads to bring his men into this focal point, if necessary. He did not like the thought, and the very real threat, of having a battle about to erupt in the seat of the King's summer court.

Preparing to leave his office in order to be with his men at the Fishgate, Braucus realized that he had reason to be somewhat optimistic about the men the King had given him. They were from the King's elite Aeonian Guard. In addition, King Ranulf Ealhhere had loaned to him High Marshall Solace Umbré's Captain, Joseph Martains. Included in the Aeonian contingent the King gave Peredurus were two sergeants, Meginhard and **Burchard.**

CHAPTER SIXTEEN

The priest had assigned his men this stormy night to monitor and patrol two central areas in the port city. About one hundred of his followers were dispatched into a dozen small neighborhoods throughout its center. Another hundred or so had been situated in the vicinity of the city safe house. When Savage had escaped from the Slake that the priest had sent into the house after him, the thaumaturge started pulling his men back toward the other group.

Yet, seeing Savage escape from the safe house, despite what he had considered were foolproof plans to kill the bowman, had put his blood up. He quickly suspended his orders of consolidating his men into the center of Seascale. Instead, he brought his safe house force back to him and let the units in the center stay in place. Mungadai had his northern group follow Savage as he progressed toward the heart of the city. He hoped to grind the bowman apart against his two bands of armed men.

About a half of a mile from the city safe house, Savage was stopped by Red. The archer was striding past a series of overhanging, second story buildings and shops that were closed for the night. It was almost pitch black. The volume of the rain, and the force of the wind pushing it, made it difficult to see much on the section of road the big man was walking. All of a sudden, a darker smudge detached itself from the side of a wall by which Savage was passing. The smudge came even with him and started talking to Savage.

"You've got a whole bunch of people following you, John."

"That doesn't surprise me, Red," Savage said with great equanimity.

Both men continued walking, until Red placed his hand firmly on the bowman's right elbow. "Don't poke me, now, with one of them double–edged stabbers you're still clutchin in those big hands of yours. We need to stop and figure out a counter strategy."

"Whadda ya have in mind?"

"You're about to be set into a vice, John. The men that were around the safe house are following you. There's got to be at least a hundred of them from what we've been able to determine over the past half a day. And, there's another group of at least the same amount, if not larger, at the center."

"Sounds about what we expected, Red. What's the problem? I'm not going through the center of the city."

153

"I understand, John; for the sake of the old King's peace of mind, listen to me."

"Red, I'm going due south to the warehouse as much as I can. There's no direct road to get there. Going this way takes me at least three to five blocks west of the center, depending on the series of alternating streets I follow to get to Mordant's place on the bay."

Red patiently wiped away the water from his face and mouth. "If I was thirsty I'd have no problem drinkin this stuff, it's comin down so fast."

"We don't have all night to stand around here in this flood jawin about it, Red," Savage drolly commented.

Even though the bowman could not see the other man's expression, Red smiled at his friend's comment. "You're not just dealin with Mordant; we are," he emphasized, "up against the priest that is at the head of the Church of Equity. It's his people that are putting this pressure on you. The northern group wants to push you toward the center so they can squash you like a bug there."

"Okay, Red, thanks for the information. It makes sense. You're providing me wise counsel. Where's Mordant and his ilk?"

"Our people reported he was at the warehouse with about fifty men."

Savage became quiet. Despite the peril facing them, they remained standing on the side of the street fully exposed to the weather and anyone looking for them.

The rain tattooed off the buildings and the road. The wind tugged at their clothes as if trying to hurry them along the way out of there.

Referring to Kosem Mungadai, Red advised, "I think you want to avoid him treating you like a cat's paw. Let's turn the tables on him."

"Okay," Savage responded, "we can exploit him, too, just like he's doing to <u>us</u>. Hold twenty men in reserve. Bring the women out first; the priest's men may be put off balance. Hard to tell, though, cause of the bad weather we're having. Have the women appear as if they just got out of church and they're walking back from the evening's service. It may allow us to put our people deeper into the territory they're holding than we could otherwise."

"Shall we start turning tables, John?"

Savage smiled at Red's use of the word tables, grimly recalling the memory of Nigel correcting the bowman's use of the word.

"Yes," the archer said. "We're doubling back toward the priest's smaller, northern force. Like our opponent, we'll split our people into two groups. You take the larger group, say fifty men, and put a perimeter at my back. Let them engage you if they move into your position. Come at them from the side, don't force them into charging your front. I'll take the smaller force of twenty–two. We'll have the advantage of surprise. We'll take them out the same way I'm advising you to do. Send two of the best runners from my group to me. You do the same at our southern line against Mungadai's folks who are in the central square area. We'll organize ourselves here and get going."

"Sounds good. Happy hunting, John."

"You as well, Red. Happy hunting."

Red turned to the side and became a smudge against the darkness once more. Soon enough, the blotch that once was a man at the bowman's side vanished into the night.

Two runners soon appeared in front of Savage. He quickly gave them his plan of battle to disseminate to the other members of the bowman's group.

Not counting the runners and himself, he divided his force into four groups with each group consisting of five people. Each group selected two people to be their own leaders or combat coordinators.

The bowman instructed them about what they were going to do. "We're looking at a territory, or battleground, of ten city blocks that lie west and northwest of the city's center. There are about a dozen streets and lanes connecting these neighborhoods together. The blocks are five abreast with one row on top of the other.

"The priest has a group at our back positioned in the central square area, which right now seems to be staying put. He's got another one positioning itself into the area I just described. We can't cover a ten-block area with the people we have. So, we're going to infiltrate the neighborhoods from the south and try to go up into the top block first.

"We'll take the five roads running in a north-south direction, so we'll be covering four city blocks. It's still too large an area. But they don't know we're taking the fight to them, or how many people we've got going against them, at least at first. Any questions?"

One of the runners responded, "Sounds like a decent plan, John. But we're going to be pressed between two forces. Where's our final point of no return?"

Savage looked at the dim outline of the runner and said, "Excellent observation! There are four streets and lanes running east to west. We'll let them converge on us in the northernmost east to west lane. It'll be tough to come at us for a variety of reasons: the overhang in the buildings and the narrowness on the street, for examples. We'll be hemmed in for sure, but we can raise havoc with them in the tight quarters. If we can't get in the top east to west lane, we'll try for the next one below, and so on. Anything else I haven't thought of?"

There was no answer, the men remained silent.

"Good. We're going to meet on Merchants Row, one block north of Center Street. There's a leatherworker's shop in between a tailor's and shoemaker's place on either side. Get everyone there as soon as you can. Let's get going."

The two runners sprang away from Savage, who then decided he would try to reconnoiter as much of the area around him that he could see, given the time he had left to get to the meeting.

The bowman took off south in ground eating strides towards Center Street.

He told himself that he just wanted to conduct reconnaissance, which he did, and effectively at that. Yet, he knew himself better. If the circumstances presented themselves with the right opportunities, he was going to create some chaos, which indeed he did.

The archer killed five men between the sweep he made of three streets while working his way over to the meeting place. He was careful whom he killed, politely asking them for whom they were working. Four of them would not tell him.

More's the favor they did me, he rationalized to himself.

One he hung from a baker's shop sign. The big man had prepared the rope before the man had shown up on that side of the street. He used part of the rope from the sign to stretch the man out on one of the two poles that helped hold the sign in place.

When the man first appeared, he had walked right up to the bowman, who dropped the rope around his neck. Savage picked him up like a sack of feathers, despite the fact that he was struggling against him. And hung him.

The next three he simply dispatched with the anelaces. He took them one at a time. Being the one to espy all three, he rapidly approached each of them. In sequential order, he took the first from the man's left side. The second he dispatched behind the man's back. The third was attacked head on.

The storm helped cloak his movements toward them.

The last one was huddled in an archway when he went by him.

Savage stopped upon seeing him there. "Oh, here you are," he said to him. "The priest wants to see you. Follow me."

Without any hesitation, the man started to follow the bowman. "Hell of a night!" he said to the big man.

Savage stopped in mid stride, turned around and grabbed the man by the back of the head with his left hand. Saying, "It sure is!" he flung him against the brick wall near the door where the other man had been standing. The man crumpled to the street wordlessly. He did not get up again.

159

No one said anything to him about being late when he arrived at the meeting place. They expected their leader would be there when he could make it. They knew the bowman was thorough in his planning and any resultant actions from it on his part were supremely justified. He showed up when he did for his own good reasons.

"Anyone around that we need to be aware of right now?" he asked all four groups.

They reported no unusual activity. A block north of where they stood, which was on Cloth Street, a few armed groups of men were stationed and in motion, walking up and down streets or lanes in their assigned areas. The enemy became more congregated at the northernmost east–west road, which was appropriately named North Street.

Savage liked what he heard. "Excellent!" he said with approval. "Our goal, first, is to swiftly take out those you saw a block north of us. Each one of our four groups takes an assigned north–south street. So, collectively, we'll be moving parallel with one another up three streets, counting the one we're on right now. Don't dally anywhere. Move up to the next cross street and converge in the middle. Two groups a piece will be going north on two streets. We converge in the center on the last cross street. Questions?"

"Suppose we get bogged down in being attacked by a superior force?"

"Scatter, vanish away in the dark before that happens. Use the storm to your advantage. Follow the plan. Converge at the next crossroad; or double back and begin again."

Mordant and his men first went in a precipitate rush back toward the city. They ran off the docks and away from the warehouse in mortal fear of the creature the Commander had placed in the building. They ran away because of the two men he had sent in after it had been been turned into ludicrously easy prey for its insatiable sensual hunger, except it was neither laughable nor easy to remain in its presence at all. No one else had any desire to be anywhere near the Slake. They were also not sure the Commander was done feeding it. No one wanted to stay and find out if that was, certainly, the case.

Having gotten ahead of Gregor Mordant, they approached the Gate of the Great Bay in indiscriminate and disorderly haste. Mordant caught up to them in, what was for him, righteous anger. The Commander rushed among them, slowed them down and made them halt at last. The fierceness of the storm made it difficult for him to be seen and heard by his men.

161

Mordant was disgusted with them. *These men are not Marauders and they certainly are not Marauder material, either.*

He finally grabbed a storm lantern from one of them and used it as a beacon to gather the men around him. Just before the entrance way of the great gate, he corralled them against its obdurate wet wall.

"Don't worry about the Slake," he shouted over the wrath of the storm. "It's not going to bother us!"

The Marauders' leader implicitly knew that Eumero had the waterfront covered. The Commander had taken all of his men with him in hopes of either catching Merek or Pall; or, failing that, rush into the priest's central group and add to the complement of men stationed there. Thus, he organized all of them into five units with each unit consisting of ten men apiece. The five men left over who were without a group, were then assigned, respectively, as the runner or messenger for each of the five groups of men.

As they went through the gate, Mordant took a deep sigh of relief in being able to get them all into a far more effective fighting force. The Great Bay Road they were on led through the center of the city towards its other encircling wall near where the safe house was located. The Commander was using this road because, from where they had passed under the gate, it was the shortest route through the city to his objective.

Each group had two lanterns. He placed one man in the front and back of each of the five groups to provide light to penetrate the murk around them. It hardly made a difference. Mordant made sure that he stayed in the middle of the light, which was just behind the first group and in between the first ranking of the first two groups on either side of him.

He had placed the most reliable and toughest men in the first group, which was in the lead and walking quickly up the middle of the road. The other four groups of men were following the first one and flanking both ends of the road, two on each side.

He took the fastest man from all the five groups and sent him into the center of the city to tell the priest they were headed his way. Walking up the middle of Great Bay Road, he did not have the courage to tell his leader that they had failed getting the two men, especially the traitor Merek, killed. The storm had leached away the color of the city and left it stained black, just like the yawning pit of fear he felt growing in the bottom of his soul.

Merek was leading Pall back toward the city safe house. Merek knew the city intimately. Thus, he was taking a diagonal route that avoided going through the city center. The route they were headed on would take them slightly west of the port city's central square. It did not matter that they had no storm lantern to light their way north. The lightning that flashed helped provide enough light for Merek to get his bearings. There also were enough homes and residences that had oil lamps or candles burning in their windows. The light given off by this source of illumination greatly helped him see where he was going.

Yet, without Merek's knowledge of Seascale, they would have been severely hampered in their progress toward the safe house.

They did not talk with one another. The storm was too loud. Neither of them wanted to shout at the other under such conditions.

Halfway between the center and the northern wall, they intermittently began to hear the sounds of fighting to the east. They stopped to listen to them for a moment. However, the storm greatly affected the acoustics of the fighting. Sometimes they could not hear anything but the pummeling of water descending on top of everything around them.

"We need to see what's going on over there, Merek," Pall urged after carefully trying to figure out just what they were hearing.

"Not a wise idea, Pall. It could be Mordant."

"I don't think so. He couldn't have caught up with us already. Besides, it's to the east of us."

"Well, it could be his men."

"True, Merek, but if we go over there to watch what's going on, we may see him join them. Then we can follow him and get him when he least expects us."

Merek did not respond.

"Look," Pall counseled, "we need to get closer. All the buildings between us and what we're hearing over there are interfering with our ability to figure out what's happening. We may be putting ourselves in further danger if we don't know who's over there."

"Okay, Pall. I'll lead the way. I know how to get us close in without being seen."

Merek was as good as his word. He brought them within half a block of the struggle they had first heard to the east. The clamor of combat became clearly evident to their senses.

Pall's military awareness and knowledge knew that a pitched battle was occurring not only in front of them, but all around the area where they had entered.

"Get ready, Merek," he cautioned his friend. "We're about to enter the fray."

Pall unstrapped the quarterstaff that had been slung on his back over his newly acquired cloak. He felt confident in himself. The thrill of hand–to–hand fighting lit into him like the lightning going off overhead.

Merek shook his head with pessimism. Despite his scruples about being where he was, he unslung the crossbow, or arbalest, that he had taken from his family's armory. Using a crank on a ratchet, he wound the string back and spanned it fully. He knew that the hempen string, which had been soaked in glue, would provide only some protection against the rain. He could release, with extreme accuracy and more than almost anyone else, two to three quarrels a minute. But he had the element of surprise on his side at this moment in time. He intended to take advantage of it. The effective range of his weapon was between three hundred fifty to four hundred yards. He also intended to take advantage of his accuracy. Merek had been taken in by Mordant partially because he was the best crossbowman the Commander had ever seen in action.

Pall was not aware of his friend's skill in handling this weapon. Merek set a bolt into the groove at the top of the crossbow's hazel wooden stock. Setting it down under the bolt clip, he made sure the nock of the quarrel was fully against the serving on the string.

The young warrior clapped him on his left shoulder and said into his ear, "There's a lookout posted underneath an overhang about a hundred feet diagonally ahead of us. Can you hit him from here without being seen?"

"Yes," answered Merek. "But whose side's he on?"

"Good question," came the response. "Take a look for yourself and tell me what you see."

Merek let Pall carefully hold the crossbow as he peered around the corner at the spot Pall indicated. He watched the man for about sixty heartbeats.

"Well, what do you think, Merek?"

In reply to Pall's question to him, Merek took his crossbow back. He stood around the corner half in and half out of sight even though the man he was aiming at could not have seen Merek. It was quite dark from where they were observing the lookout. Merek rested his thumb on the first of the three notches and lined the bolt with his thumb which formed his sight. He took a breath and as he let it out, the trigger was pulled.

A sharp report went off from the weapon as the bolt was released.

Lightning flashed as soon as the bolt penetrated and went through the man's neck.

"Merek," Pall said aloud in a normal voice, forgetting where he was at the moment, "that's one wicked shot!"

"Thanks, Pall."

"But why did you risk shooting the man?"

"Oh, I knew him. He was one of Mordant's Marauders."

Captain Martains and his seventy–five men had been assigned by Braucus to the north central side of the wall at Kingsgate. Martains' sphere of control was near the priest's city safe house. They were already in position at Kingsgate. As Dolphin Street, running in a direct north–south route, directly connected with Fishgate and Kingsgate, Peredurus used cavalry to relay information back and forth between both groups. If a battle erupted in the center of the city, as he speculated it would, the Kingsgate contingent was in easy reach of Guild Street to get there because it branched off Dolphin Street within half a mile of the gate. The men stationed temporarily at Fishgate could be quickly moved to the center by going about two–thirds of a mile north on Dolphin Street where they could turn left on Grail Street. This street led into the center of the port city.

The Minister was chafing over the fact that he did not have the number of men that he believed was necessary to contain those of Mungadai and Mordant's. He had wanted at least another five hundred men.

Captain Martains, reluctantly, had agreed with the Minister that if, indeed, there was an armed force of men in the city equal to the numbers Peredurus had quoted him, they would need the additional manpower to cordon off, or sequester, them. The Captain was taking a dim view of this assignment, especially being out in the night at the mercy of the foulest weather they had experienced in the summer to date. He thought he was simply here to mollify the paranoia of the King's Minister of Affairs.

Had he the full resources of the army, he would have just gone through the city the way beaters in the fields flush out deer or any game worth shooting, round them up and throw them into the King's dungeons where they could sit for the rest of eternity, for all he cared.

Thus, when a rider arrived at Fishgate from Peredurus, Martains was not quick to respond to the warning given in the message from Braucus. Reports going to the Minister were filled with alarm over fighting erupting just northwest of the city square. As they were live action reports that were orally transmitted by runners to the Minister, it was difficult for Martains to determine their validity. Plus, these were civilian dispatches for which he held even further suspicion and disdain as well.

The Minister wanted the Captain to begin moving into position and to have his men well on their way up Grail Street toward the center of the city.

Martains concluded that the better strategy was to stay below the arch of the gate under which he was already standing. He did not relish going out into the pouring rain to engage in an ephemeral goose chase, especially on the basis of undependable communiques.

In the meantime, Peredurus had ridden south for a tenth of a mile and turned right onto Guild Street with his contingent of one hundred twenty–five men. He was under the assumption that Martains was doing the same, but south of, and converging, with the Minister onto the city square. Braucus intended to put a screen of men between the priest's forces and the eastern part of the city.

"At least," he muttered aloud to himself, "I can contain the disaster in the northwest from bleeding over towards the King's quarters in the southeastern section of the city."

He also thought that he would be able to check any aid to the enemy coming from the east or from the south. *That will help Savage deal with the numbers already arrayed against him and not compound the challenge facing him.*

The wind howled around him as he rode his horse at the head of his men.

His men walked down the street more like a mob of vigilantes than an organized unit of intelligence.

Peredurus did not mind their sullenness. He wanted them angry for what was about to happen. He intended to use their emotions effectively in order to fuel their ability to kill the priest's men.

CHAPTER SEVENTEEN

Kosem Mungadai was frustrated, bemused and angry over Savage's disappearance.

For years, he had prided himself on his ability to glean, sift through and gain intelligence over those he wished to conquer and rule. A report had been brought to him that the archer was seen talking to someone else on a street not far south of the city safe house. The man talking with Savage had faded into the night and was not able to be followed. Two other men joined Savage, and after speaking with him, left. These men were followed, but then were lost, as well, into the night.

Savage vanished into the murkiness of the storm and the evening. However, some of the priest's men were being killed in three areas. Two were on the east–west streets of Merchant and Cloth, while the third was in the vicinity of Butcher's Row, a north–south lane where it intersected with North Street.

The priest was confused, at first, over these deaths because he could not see how Savage could have been the perpetrator of them all.

Mungadai was angry over the fact that first blood had been drawn against him. He had followers who were knifed, hung from a sign post and bludgeoned in the head. Others were shot in the neck by a bolt from a crossbow, had their throats slit or simply disappeared. Two were found drowned in tubs of water that were reserved for fighting fire. Containers like them were placed on the streets throughout the city. They were rarely used for the purpose they were meant to serve and mostly filled with garbage and rubbish.

It was the latter thought of his men's bodies being put in putrid water filled with refuse that raised his ire to a white–hot incandescence. He decided to put two of his assistants in charge of his forces; one, Abagha Zhenjin, was to oversee the northern force, while the other, Altan Esender, was to supervise the southern one.

Mungadai went back to his monastery. He went to take the special hallucinogenic potion he used to prepare for entering his scrying chamber. However, none was ready for him to take. Eager to get into the chamber, and with the understanding that he was running out of time, he hastily made a fresh batch of stimulant. He called it by several names, depending upon with whom he was talking about it. However, he thought of it as his naijé, or his "give–me" elixir.

This evening, he put together a more than potent mixture of ingredients containing mushrooms, cinnabar, seeds, root bark and select fork–rooted plants. To speed the process of his divination, he added the few remaining leaves of salvia he had left in his private apothecary. Mashing the ingredients in a mortar and pestle, he rashly combined them into half a cup of mead.

Finished with these preparations, he downed the drink in one long sustained series of gulps. The priest stripped all his clothes off and entered his chamber. It took him a while to settle down and even more to clear away his thoughts and emotions. He had not bothered to light any lamps or candles. He knew this room better than his own body. He knew its vagaries and nuances, as well as its ambiance and personality under all sorts of conditions and circumstances.

It took more time for the mirrors to register the presence of the darknesses he was summoning. When they did come to him, they came as shadows streaking across the sweep of the mirrors in the room overhead. Like the harp strings being strummed by an archangel of hell, they screamed their vengeance at him.

He roared his defiance and wrath back at them. Their combined voices merged into a shriek of dismaying dissonance whose decibel level popped the priest's ear drums. Blood flowed from his ears onto his shoulders. Claws reached out from the fount of water before him, trying to touch and absorb the blood pooling into it. One set grabbed the priest by the jaw and held him fast against the marbled rim. A wind arose in the chamber and jabbered in foreign tongues at the corners of the room.

Above Mungadai, in the room overhead, shapes started to form.

Fifteen Slakes, fifteen Üngers, and fifteen each of assorted imps, jinns and demons came into being.

They could sense below, in the room underneath, the priest's thoughts—interwoven with his maniacal laughter—rising up and telling them where they must go on this world to defeat his enemies.

His men arrived at the center of the city on a timely basis. They entered the square with military precision. Mordant was proud of them, especially seeing as how they had fallen apart on the waterfront in reaction to the Slake let loose in the priest's warehouse.

Altan Esender, the monk appointed by the priest to be in charge of this southern force, had been expecting them. He used all of Mordant's force to replace fifty of his own men. The fifty men he released from their positions around the center square were sent north to help reinforce those fighting northwest of their original position.

175

Information coming back to Esender from the battle erupting up ahead of them sounded desperate. The priest's force there was being torn apart by hit and run tactics.

Even worse news was that Kosem Mungadai had disappeared. No one had seen him for well over an hour now.

He brought Mordant up to date about what was happening and what the monk was planning on doing.

"I'd go with my men, but Brother Mungadai put me here; and, it is here I must stay," he informed the Commander. "We are to wait for the signal to push ahead in order to grind the scum we are battling to a pulp against our brothers moving down from the city safe house towards us."

Mordant streamed the water pouring down from the skies away from his eyes. Light from storm lanterns held by men around them lit up his features. He looked exhausted. "Can we talk about this under that arch over there?" he asked. "I need a break from feeling like I am a perpetually drowning rat."

Esender shrugged his shoulders indifferently at the Commander's question. However, he accompanied Mordant to the arch without visible or audible protest.

Gregor sighed deeply once he was out of the brunt of the storm. He reviewed what occurred at the warehouse, mentioning that the use of the Slake had not been fulfilled. Two of his own men had died instead. He described who Pall and Merek were and asked Esender if he, or his men, had seen the two young men.

"No, nothing has been seen of such people as you describe them," he responded to Mordant's question. "But we had the same results with the Slake my brother put into the city safe house to go after the big man called Savage."

Mordant did not make a comment.

A messenger appeared and approached Esender. The man stopped at the edge of the lantern light and waited to be acknowledged.

"Proceed," the monk curtly ordered.

"Master Esender," the runner intoned. "I am the last one sent to you from our brothers northwest of here. Have any others reached you recently?"

The monk shook his head, "No, my son. What do you need to tell me?"

"We are not faring well. Savage and his men, women fighters included, are tearing into us and we cannot seem to withstand their power. They seem like the storm pressing onto us. We cannot punch the rain or catch the wind. How do you fight such wraiths? We need your people to start pressing Savage's back."

Esender received the runner's news with cool detachment. The monk also was not bothered by his messenger's perplexity concerning the bowman's fighting tactics.

"Have you seen or heard from Brother Mungadai?" he asked.

"No, Brother Esender. No one has. But Abagha Zhenjin, who was appointed by our leader to command the city safe house force, begs you to bring your men forward."

Altan Esender bowed his head and remained quiet for a moment, as though he was trying to communicate telepathically with his senior priest.

Raising his head at the messenger before him, he straightforwardly stated, "We will do so. Return to Brother Zhenjin and tell him we will be reinforcing him momentarily."

The monk turned to Mordant. "Commander, you and your men will remain here until further notice. You are to hold this position at all costs."

The monk signed the messenger away from him, and without further comment to Mordant, stepped away toward his men. Esender gave a high piercing whistle to which all of his men in the immediate area responded. He sent for the others, and within a short time all of them were present.

Esender gave them his orders and then led them northwest of the city square.

Mordant looked around him with pessimism. He did not like what was happening. His Marauders' senses were telling him to get out of there. Yet, he remained in place.

"Yet for a little while," he said to the storm.

The rain poured down from the heavens as if it never intended to stop. Thunder cracked overhead.

Pall and Merek turned into an effective sniping team. Pall acted as an observer while Merek picked off the targets Pall selected. The young warrior also acted as the lookout for the pair. Merek had knocked off nine men thus far.

The two had gone within three blocks southwest of the city safe house, and turned back towards the fighting, approaching it from a northwest angle. Thus, they unknowingly attacked the priest's northern force from a different direction than Savage.

Pall was exhilarated at Merek's stunning skill with the crossbow. "I understand that even a young lad can aim this thing," he said to Merek, patting the weapon with respect when it was still unloaded. "But you bring it to a level of deadly precision I have never seen, my friend."

Merek said, half apologetically, "I only have about another thirty to forty quarrels left in my quiver."

Pall laughed, "I think we can do a lot of damage with those remaining bolts."

With the priest missing, his northern force faltered and, without his inspiration overseeing their fighting morale and performance, they were taking a very bad beating. Red's group, attacking them fiercely from the south, put them into a reverse position wherein they were dealt with what they hoped would be done to Savage. Red was almost completely able to stop any messages from getting to Altan Esender's southern group, thus stalling them into a holding position.

Red's force, by avoiding any sustained combat, concentrated on picking off their opponents piecemeal. The psychological damage on Abagha Zhenjin's group of a hundred men was devastating. He had lost about a third of his men. Rumors were flying throughout Zhenjin's men that a crossbowman was effectively shutting them down on their northwestern side.

The combined force of Savage's and Red's tactics, along with the unnerving sniper attacks onto his left flank, made the monk decide to pull his men away from the zone of combat. Consequently, Savage's and Red's forces came together while Zhenjin's escaped on mostly the eastern side.

A brief celebration occurred when they met one another in the middle of Cloth Street.

"Excellent work, John!" Red congratulated the bowman.

"You as well, Red!" both men laughed.

Savage turned serious. "We've got to get back to work. It'll get serious now. The men we were fighting have collapsed back to the square and joined the force that has been held in position there. We'll be dealing with two hundred men."

Both leaders did a head count and discovered that Savage had lost five men. Red lost eleven. Their two groups, formerly having seventy–people, had been whittled down to fifty–six.

"What do you suggest we do now, John?"

"Stay here and let them come to us. We know the area better than before. We have escape routes on three sides of us now. Let's split ourselves up into eight groups, seven in each one. We put five into play and leave two in reserve."

"Okay, sounds good. How do you want us in position?"

"We'll go back to North Street; give them a greater distance to move over to get uncomfortable about. We can hover in their front using an arc formation, but it all has to remain fluid like before."

"What about using the other two groups to squeeze down on them onto their left and right sides? If we can get behind them, we can do two separate crushing movements on them, then work into the middle of them."

"Sounds feasible, Red; but, they've got two hundred men to throw at us. Let's see how they go about doing it, initially. We'll figure it out from there. We've got to stay fluid like water in a river."

Red snorted at the simile. "I'm beginning to think I'm a duck from being in it this long already."

Eight groups were formed. They were given their orders of battle. They elected two leaders for each group. Everyone knew what they had to do.

They went back to North Street in the midst of the storm.

His men were within three good throws of a javelin to the city square. The storm's intensity had lessened, but he did not think it would continue that way.

Asking his men to form a large circle, Peredurus instructed them on how they were going to proceed against Mungadai's men.

"Select five of the best men to be our runners. Forget using horses, it's too dangerous, too dark and too slippery on the streets to use them. Tie the horses off in a safe place; we'll get them later. Once you're done, we're dividing into five groups, twenty–four to a group. We'll be marching one block south of Center Street and form up there. Captain Martains should be there now, or will be arriving there shortly. He'll organize his men in a similar manner as we have done already.

Once we're in place, we turn north and start pushing back the men that are on the north side of the street. We'll continue this movement until we reach the defensive wall beyond North Street."

A bolt of lightning jabbed through the sky overhead. Oddly enough, no thunder followed it.

The Minister and his men turned away from heading into the city center and followed the Minister's directions as he had shared with them.

They arrived onto Crafts Street, one block south of Center Street. Martains and his men were not already there; they were not even in sight. The Minister sent two runners to find the Captain. They were to return the way they came in to Crafts Street, but to turn right onto Grail Street. Braucus told them to go all the way back to Fishgate if they had to until they located the Captain.

"Tell him his presence was desired over an hour ago! He is to move here immediately and follow us north from Center Street. He is to sweep up the first five blocks west of the city square. It is important that he join our forces together."

Immediately after the two runners left to find Captain Martains, Peredurus moved his men north in the manner he had prescribed to them.

Reaching Center Street, they paused at their respective intersections before moving fully onto this road. Braucus sent men up singly to scout out what, or who, was in front of them. These scouts returned saying that an undetermined number of men was haphazardly gathered on the other side of Center Street. They were amassed over a three-block area.

"If you were to hazard a guess at their numbers, what figure would you give me?" he asked his advance spotters.

Their answers ranged from seventy to a hundred men.

The Minister reconfigured the movement of his force. "We're still going to stay in our formations, but we're going to deploy them as follows: three groups will move right up the center into them. The middle group stays within the center block and overwhelms the men in that area. The groups on the left and right take care of the blocks on either side of the center one. Groups four and five will take the outside blocks from the side and will roll them up into the middle. I want groups four and five out first. When you're in position, shoot an arrow into the sign above me. When two arrows are there, you're to push into the left and right blocks with full force from the side you're attacking, while the three central groups will rush across Center Street and engage who's there. The three groups with me will charge when you hear me hit a javelin butt end first onto the door in back of me."

Braucus urged the men in groups four and five onward and waited for their signal to charge forward across Center Street.

The wind picked up slightly.

The rain fell a bit harder.

Lightning flared.

Two arrows almost simultaneously hit the sign above his head.

Braucus Peredurus had the man next to him rap the nearby door three times as hard as he could.

Seventy–eight men silently, ominously and resolutely crossed Center Street in a determined rush. They ran directly into fifty–six men.

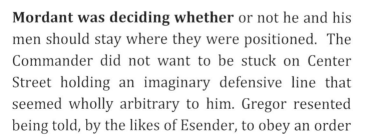

Mordant was deciding whether or not he and his men should stay where they were positioned. The Commander did not want to be stuck on Center Street holding an imaginary defensive line that seemed wholly arbitrary to him. Gregor resented being told, by the likes of Esender, to obey an order given to him second or thirdhand. If Kosem Mungadai wanted him to do something, then the priest should be the one to tell him directly. That was the way he had worked with the thaumaturge ever since he started associating with him. He did not like being someone else's lackey.

Mordant also did not think he was situated in a sound position. He was uncomfortable being there to the point of having a presentiment, or foreboding, of disaster. The Commander wanted to move his men from the position in which they had peremptorily been put. He started thinking strategically of ways to exit away from there.

Across the street from where he stood, he heard someone knocking sharply on a door three times. Before he was able to determine what the sound represented, the shapes of men appeared from out of the rain in front of him and attacked his position.

His men were ill–prepared for this attack. Men on either side of his flanks tried to escape up and down the streets. They were prevented by other attacking forces coming from the very places into which they wanted to flee.

Within minutes of being overwhelmed, he had lost eleven men. The rest, including the Commander, surrendered.

When he was brought before the head of the assaulting force against him, he was shocked to discover it was the King's Minister of Affairs, Braucus Peredurus.

The two runners Peredurus sent to find Captain Joseph Martains not only went past the city's central square and down Grail Street to find him, they ended up at the Fishgate where the Captain had remained in place since the beginning of his assignment to help the Minister. They found the Captain in a very vexed frame of mind.

To their surprise, as well as to the Captain's credit, Martains abruptly changed his attitude from annoyance to alacrity, especially when he heard that armed men against the Crown were arrayed in the western part of Center Street. Galvanized into action by this latest news, he got his elite force into sudden and effective motion.

Burchard and Meginhard quickly translated the Captain's orders into immediate execution. Within minutes of receiving the Minister's runners, and listening to their messages, the Aeonians were marching rapidly up Dolphin Street.

Merek did not run out of bolts shooting at his opponents, he ran out of opponents to shoot, instead. The sounds of fighting had stopped. The storm even lessened momentarily in its intensity.

"Let's head back to Mordant's city safe house," he suggested to Pall. "It would make sense that he would go back into his own familiar neighborhood."

"Makes sense to do that, but I think we should first discover who it is that's fighting against Mordant's men."

"Okay, Pall, that's a good idea."

"You took out nine men, Merek. And we know, from finding other bodies and those who were wounded trying to get away from the fighting on the streets, that the men going up against Mordant were well commanded. Let's nose around a bit and see if we can determine whose side we've been helping. You know this area probably as good as, or even better than, Mordant does. What do you suggest we do?"

Merek gave some thought to Pall's question before replying. "I think they know we're here, Mordant's men that is. Sooner or later, they'll come looking for us. The people in the other force may also know or suspect we're here, too.

I think we should head east and get on the other side of them. Once we get there, we can briefly split up: I'll go north, you south, to see what's in front and back of us. Or, because doing that presents a serious problem of being dangerously separated from one another, we can both do it, but it'll take longer. We don't have much time to do that."

"Okay, how about we observe who's north of us as we get to the eastern side of the fighting? That way when we get on the other side, we can both check to the south of us?"

"Hadn't thought of that, Pall. Sounds good! And we'll save even more time if we did it separately like I first thought of doing."

The two men set out to accomplish their new goal.

The rain pouring down upon them vacillated between a miserable drizzle and an execrable deluge. Thunder boomed to their south.

As they proceeded east, they angled north and soon discovered groups of men massed in an arc facing south on North Street. Pall was surprised at their light numbers.

Due to the darkness of the night, and the hindrance of the rain and wind making it harder to discern what they were seeing, they could not determine who was in this contingent force of men.

Upon reaching Iron Street, Merek headed south. "This street parallels the Great Bay Road, which connects directly with the city center. We have to be careful going down it. So, I'm only going to stay on it for a bit. Then, we'll go down Metal Row. It's a very narrow lane. You have to know it well to use it. I don't think an opposing force of men would want to be caught in there as it's too tight for fighting."

"Load your crossbow now before we get in there," Pall advised as he unslung the quarterstaff from his back. "How's the string holding up in this damp?"

"Nothing to worry about," Merek replied, as he prepared to draw the string with the winder. "I brought seven strings. I keep the spares wrapped around my waist. I've gone through three already."

Once prepared, they started down the alley. Merek was in the lead to give him room to release the quarrel when needed. The tall buildings on either side of the lane were three or four stories high. They were stacked tightly against one another. Each building was no more than eighteen to twenty feet wide, thereby providing for a greater number of merchants to have frontage on the street. Facing the road side first allowed merchants to have their shop frontage viewed by passersby at the street level. As all the shops were closed, hinged wooden barricades had been battened down over the windows when the owners closed their stores for the end of their day's business.

Most of the windows were shuttered due to the storm. Almost none of them were glazed, making the shutters play an even more important role in protecting the interior of the buildings. Each store employed heavy oaken doors that were shut and locked by sliding wooden bolts on the inside.

The owners and their families lived on the floors above their shops.

Merek and Pall were walking by heavily and sturdily protected enterprises, which made the young men feel even more exposed and isolated away from the people living within these structures.

Merek suddenly veered off the lane. He took several turnings onto a series of back alleys until Pall, who had an excellent sense of direction, became confused as to where they were headed.

The crossbowman came to a halt in an alley that was no wider than five feet. The rain barely landed on them because the jetties of the upper stories almost brushed against one another across the roadway.

"I've taken us to the heart of the neighborhood. We're just four or five blocks away from Center and Iron streets. The city center is southeast of us," Merek informed Pall.

"Can you take me around this area through these paths so I can learn how to navigate through them?"

"Yes," Merek answered. "I think this is an excellent place to be. We can fight off an army in here."

"How do you know this area so well?"

"I spent a lot of time here when I was a boy, throughout the entire city, actually."

Merek spent the next half hour teaching Pall the directional intricacies of the streets, alleys, rows and lanes in which they were intending to fight.

In the process of absorbing the seemingly random geometry of the space they were in, they heard men moving over the wider streets going south past their position.

When they were able to spy on them, Merek identified them as Mordant's group of people. These men seemed dispirited, desultory. No one talked. They walked wearily by, continually looking over their shoulders behind them. Those holding storm lanterns did so carelessly as though carrying them in their hands was an afterthought only.

After they passed by where the two young men were hidden, Merek said, "The people we saw in formed groups on North Street must have been the ones that gave those just going by us a whipping. I think the men that went by us now are going to join up with another group south of us. It's a standard tactic that Marauders use. They weren't running away. They were purposefully walking towards a link–up."

"All the more reason to get me to learn this neighborhood as thoroughly, and as fast, as you can finish teaching me, Merek."

Pall was an adept student and quick learner. He had an eidetic, unerring memory for such things.

The northern group of men that met their southern counterparts coming towards them was a dispirited one. Yet, just before these men came into contact with their fellow believers, their attitude started changing from feeling defeated to becoming morose, sour, and then simply angry. Moving through the main streets as though they were seeing them for the first time, they could not understand what had just happened to them.

What has become of our master? Many of them were asking in their hearts. *He has never deserted us.*

Kosem Mungadai, the father of them all, was never defeated; he was always triumphant in his efforts and desires to expand the influence of his beliefs on others. He, aided by the power of his spiritual covenant, invariably vanquished whomever and whatever opposed him and his believers. The priest was a paragon of indomitable strength. For them, he had become an apotheosis; he was transcendence at the highest level anyone could attain. And this immortal had given them the faith they had in him; the promises he had made to them, the eternal life he said was available to those worshipping him, was also theirs, and belonged to them by right of the sacrifices each one of them had made in following him.

They aspired to be gods, too, exactly like their Father. Such a desideratum formed an implacable ambition that was set in stone in the deepest part of their being. It became a just, and a righteous, path to follow, with the inevitable understanding that some were on the verge of being demigods—even now at this present moment in time.

When Abagha Zhenjin and his band of men made contact with their peers, it was they who inspired Altan Esender and his men.

"Our Father is praying and interceding for us with the darknesses that love him so," Zhenjin said to Esender. We must turn back and smash these heathens into the dust of their heresy."

The two leaders hugged and kissed one another on each cheek in their ritual, ceremonial greeting. To a man, they knelt down on their knees and prayed to Mungadai for deliverance from their oppressors.

Arising from their due deference, genuflection and invocation to their father priest, they turned back north. A gleam was in their eyes. An impassioned sense of power was in their hearts. They were not just followers and fanatics burning with the fever of justification in their spirits. These men—all one hundred ninety–five of them—were indomitable, they were conquerors, they had already won the battle over the soul of this city.

Mordant was disgusted for being caught in a trap of another man's mistakes. *I should have gotten the hell out of here when I first was told to stay at all costs*, he groused to himself.

He and his men had been put in bunches of threes. Only those wounded seriously were not tied up and placed roughly against the storefront walls on the north side of Center Street. The Commander's hands were bound tightly behind his back. His feet were also bound by rope. He had been put roughly on the street next to where Peredurus sat on his horse.

The rain had gotten its strength back and was incessantly pouring down upon him. Mordant was mad, miserable and malcontent with his lot.

The Minister ignored him.

Lightning arched in webbed striations of searing light in the sky over the street.

Thunder cracked, boomed in anger.

Mordant started laughing.

Shapes reared up at the east end of Center Street.

The Commander, in a cachinnation that bellowed up from the bottom of his own anger, and amongst his raucous laughter, saw at least ten Slakes coming toward them.

Peredurus tried ignoring the King's favorite spy who was sitting in misery on the street almost underneath the feet of his horse.

He wanted to question Gregor, but there was no suitable place to do it, especially out in the middle, or even on the side, of the street. The Minister wanted to know if Mordant had been in contact with Savage, what forces were opposing the King and their disposition.

The rain became relentless.

The wind blew by in powerful blasts.

Lightning and thunder discharged in simultaneous display of the storm's dominance over the men in the street.

Mordant's laughter rose up at Braucus, settling onto him like a fervid wetness.

With alarm, the Minister saw that all the men, his and Mordant's, were huddled against the buildings. He was about to order his men away and back out into the street. However, before he could do so, Mordant's chortling turned into a shriek of madness as lightning went off in an aerial series of powerful kinetic explosions.

Astride his horse, whose shoulders stood at fifteen hands above the street, Braucus had an excellent view of the road in both directions in which it ran. Following Mordant's gaze, Peredurus saw eleven women purposefully walking down the street towards him.

Unalarmed, he waited for them to get within conversational distance from where he sat on his horse. When they were fifty feet away, his horse started snorting and acting as though wasps were attacking it. It started to buck uncontrollably. The Minister was a superb horseman. Yet, the instantaneous change in conditions that was occurring all around him unsettled him. The horse's fear took command and overwhelmed his rider's control over the animal.

As the women, undeterred by the large horse dancing dangerously in front of them, continued approaching, Braucus' horse sped away in the opposite direction, carrying his stunned rider far to the west of where he had previously stood.

Ten women flowed around the laughing man sitting on the street in the pouring rain. One stopped before him. She reached out with her hand and lifted up the man's chin. Her desire for him was so great that she started emitting heat waves that palpably radiated over him. The rain pelting down on the pair of them was evaporated as it touched them.

Mordant screamed. There was no more merriment in his voice, but a roaring snicker that turned into yowling. He mewled, puled and whined, which turned into a whisper, whose sound was soon overcome by the severity of the storm.

The Slake literally glowed with the heat of absorbing the Commander's energy. Suffused with the mortal's vitality she had just imbibed whole, she pushed him away from her and started walking, almost nonchalantly, towards those mortals still awaiting her ardent and fatal salacity for them.

As Gregor Mordant's body fell against the street, it turned to dust. The rain washed it away in a smear of wet grime that streamed toward the men hunched against the storefronts. But these men did not have the luxury of watching what had happened in front of them.

They had their own worries to deal with instead.

The contagion of fear, as well as the eruption of false eroticism that erupted from the presence of the Slakes, literally forced many of Peredurus' men away from where they had been clumped together against the buildings. They saw what was happening to those men subject to the Slakes' sexual predation.

Their stamina for battle was stripped completely away. They were bereft of courage.

They ran without thought of where they were headed.

Mordant's men could not do so. They were fixed in place by the ropes binding them into the spots where they had been set.

The injured tried crawling away to no avail.

Eleven Slakes soon realized the purpose of their creation. Consuming the number of men still left on the side of the street took time.

Such evil enjoyed every moment of it.

CHAPTER EIGHTEEN

A large number of men, ten of whom were holding lighted storm lanterns before them, started moving by the two young men who were hiding within the darkness of a small alley that emptied onto Iron Street.

Merek and Pall waited until the last group passed by them.

There were no stragglers.

Both young fighters noted that this group of men carried themselves differently than the one they had just recently observed going south.

"They've got reinforcements," Merek whispered to Pall.

"Let's follow them and see if we can pick off some that were last to go by us."

"Okay, Pall, but we need to be sure that, when we attack, we have a way to go back into the neighborhood I just showed you."

Pall answered his ally by patting the palm of his hand twice on top of Merek's left shoulder.

Pulling away from the cover of the buildings that overhung the warren of lanes, alleys and paths Pall had been learning, fully exposed them not only to discovery, but to the full force of the storm as it seemed to have renewed itself with powerful surges of wind, rain, lightning and its accompanying thunder against the city and its residents.

Merek decided to head the group of men off by taking a sequence of back alleys that ran diagonally ahead of their route. The two fighters, consequently, arrived before the first men in the group reached where Merek and Pall had chosen to ambush them. Merek had already spanned the arbalest and loaded it with a fresh quarrel.

They patiently waited until the last of the men passed by and the light from the lantern he held almost completely faded from sight. The men were going slightly uphill. When the last man passed by him, Merek stepped onto the street and aimed the crossbow at him. His target was still outlined by the light of the storm lantern being carried by another man who was near the head of his group. Thunder was rolling sharply above them and it obscured the sound of the bolt being released from the crossbow.

Merek shot the man through the neck. At such close range, the energy propelling the bolt went through him without being impeded whatsoever. The quarrel lodged deeply in the back of the man ahead of him.

The second man uttered a cry of surprise mingled with that of pain, but his cry of mortal dismay was not heard; it was smothered by a violent burst of thunder.

Two men, lifeless, were down onto the street.

Two more men were singly dispatched in the same manner.

The third time Merek shot the crossbow, the string snapped in half upon the release of the bolt. The missile went wild and caromed off the side of the building near another man.

Fifteen men came to a halt on this man's warning shout.

They looked in back of them, but could not see anyone. The man carrying the storm lantern completely shuttered its light.

Holding a hurried conversation, they agreed it was not worth chasing after someone they could not see. No other bolts were fired. No other offensive moves were made against them. They ran forward away from their invisible foe as rapidly and as safely as they could in the rain and in the dark of night.

When the elite Aeonian fighters reached the halfway mark towards the Minister's last reported position, Martains sent three runners ahead to reconnoiter the area and to make contact with Peredurus himself. They were told to remain with him until the main unit arrived.

Thus, it was with some surprise and consternation that all three runners came back just as Martains' unit was reaching Central Square. The Captain called his men to a halt upon the runners' appearance.

After hearing what they conveyed to him about the strange slaughter occurring just to the west of them on Center Street, Martains decided not to split his force in half. He moved west out onto Crafts Street to bypass the area where he had expected to meet Peredurus. Nearing the first north–south intersection, he sent men one block up to Center Street to see what they could find. Nothing unusual was observed, other than the sounds of screaming east of them where the massacre was occurring.

Reaching the second such intersection, he found some of the Minister's men walking around in a stupefied and bewildered fashion. It took some coaxing, reassuring and patience to get a more complete story from them about what had happened. The Captain sent more of his men in a grid search six blocks wide and four blocks deep with Center Street being set in the middle of it. He placed Sergeant Burchard in charge of those in the northern sector, and Sergeant Meginhard to lead similar efforts in the southern. Eventually, they came back with almost all of the men who had fled the scene. Not counting the Minister, an even dozen was missing.

Gathering these men around him, he walked with them towards the fifth intersection. To his delight, Peredurus was astride his still nervous horse waiting for them to reach him.

Holding a brief conference together, in which they also involved the Minister's men, they devised a plan of attack. Martains recommended they proceed in force to North Street towards the priest's safe house. He and the Minister would cross Center Street and alternately lead their men north up Butchers and Farmers streets. They intended to converge together on North Street and, at that point, create a blueprint for attacking the safe house. Meginhard was assigned to Peredurus. Burchard remained with the Captain.

The storm continued unabated as they crossed Center Street.

Each group headed towards its assigned route.

Fifty–six men, gathered in eight groups containing seven men each, stood silently waiting in the downpour, either for a signal from their two leaders to attack, or for the priest's men to come out of the darkness and attack them. Six groups were ranged in a semi–circle with one extra group on either side forming a slight flange on their arched formation.

Red was in front at the center of the arch.

Placed opposite Red, right behind the concaved tip of the arch, was Savage. He stood on a roughly constructed stand his men had assembled for him. The stand, being four feet high, combined with the archer's height, brought his view way above the backs of the men. He commanded a perspective that was almost eleven feet off the ground.

His seven-foot long bow was still unstrung; the string remained wrapped loosely around his waist. Seven broadhead arrows, fletched with his signature design of two barred green hens and a solid blue vane for the middle feather, were placed neatly in front of him. He had three sheaves, or bundles, of arrows in reserve, waiting for him to use. Each sheave consisted of twenty-six arrows whose length measured thirty-six inches apiece. Counting the thirty in his quiver, the bowman had just over a hundred arrows to use.

Lightning seared across the sky revealing to Savage that the priest's forces had entered the combat area he and Red had picked earlier. They unhurriedly amassed together in preparation for a charge. Storm lanterns were unshuttered and set down on the road among them.

Red turned around and spoke to Savage saying, "They seem too comfortable for my liking, John."

"That's cause they got somethin else going on," responded the archer as he strung the longbow. "I think they're going to be reinforced. Keep sharp, now. Let them come to us."

The wind picked up from the northeast driving the rain ahead of it.

Savage took time to nock an arrow to the bow-string. He was assessing the conditions under which he had to shoot. Once the arrow was ready to be drawn on its string, the bowman pressed all of his weight into the horns of his bow. He steadied his aim onto one man who stood in front of one of the lanterns. He adjusted his aim for the windage. The big man released the arrow, which was impelled by one hundred eighty pounds of contained force from his longbow.

The arrow flew true, striking the man in the center of his chest. He flopped to the street. The men standing around their now dead comrade applauded the lethal elegance of the archer's shot.

This applause did not unnerve Red, it made him angry instead.

The ovation did not disturb Savage either. He comfortably released five more arrows into them within a two minute span. Four of the missiles knocked down their intended targets. A fifth man fell, but the bowman could not account for that as he knew that his sixth arrow had gone wide of the mark.

Someone else is shooting at them besides me. Good, we need to get rid of as many of them as we can right now.

206

Applause rippled among the priest's men again. However, they shuttered their storm lanterns.

The bowman placed six more arrows in front of him. He set another arrow onto his bowstring and prepared to shoot. He waited for lightning to strike. The priest's men stayed unmoved in their assigned positions.

Lightning flared. Another man fell in the rear ranks.

The bowman shot another arrow into the priest's men.

Savage's men sternly looked ahead of them.

In the bosom of the night's obscurity, two opposing forces stood poised for battle.

"There are no more shortcuts to head them off," Merek said to Pall, "especially at the increased speed they just made in getting away from us. We may as well go all the way to North Street and see if we can get behind them there."

Pall did not answer. He simply followed Merek through more back alleys and lanes.

They were almost at the end of their journey through these obscure byways when they reached Iron Street.

"We're one block south of North Street," Merek informed Pall.

207

"We'll be more exposed on these main streets. Can we walk between buildings to get up there while still having more cover?"

"No, the buildings are right next to each other on North Street cause frontage is important to the merchants."

"Then let's stay on the left side of this street till we get there. If we need to get out of there, we can retreat back this way and head into the alleys again."

Merek was about to respond to Pall's last comment, but Pall interrupted him.

"I just had an idea, Merek. You said the buildings are too tightly built together, making it impossible to get through them."

"That's right," Merek concurred.

"Can we get on top of those buildings?"

"Sure, we used to...." Merek stopped in mid statement. He understood what Pall was thinking about. "What a great idea, Pall! Follow me."

Merek took Pall back into the alley where they had walked onto Iron Street. He took a right onto a pathway that was only three feet wide. They squeezed by buildings that were less than two feet apart in several places. Pall had to take hold of his sword and quarterstaff in his hands to fit through them.

They had to crawl through the last one. An oil lantern shining out of a window close by helped light the area through which they were trying to pass. Merek untied the extra crossbow strings at his waist. He emptied all of the bolts out of his quiver, pulling out a cloth that was stuffed in the bottom. He put the strings in the middle of the cloth, rewrapped them in it, stuffed it back down into the base of the quiver and put all the bolts back in as well.

"Please set this on the crossbow before you crawl through, and push it on ahead carefully."

Pall handed his weapons to Merek and then took the crossbow and quiver that Merek handed over to him in return, placing them onto the cloak he had just taken off. Pushing the cloak wrapped weapons ahead of him, he wormed his way through the constricted space, getting soaking wet in the process.

The young soldier stood up once he made it to the other side. He checked the condition of the arbalest and quiver, and found them undamaged and in good shape. He informed Merek he could start out and that the crossbowman's weapons were in excellent order.

Merek took off his own cloak and placed Pall's weapons on it. The crossbowman made it through just fine, being sure to push the cloak and Pall's weapons carefully ahead of him.

Once on the other side, Pall helped Merek to his feet. They exchanged their weapons with one another.

As Merek was draping his cloak back on, Pall said, "Seems a shame to ruin such fine cloth."

"Better to ruin such than not have our arms intact," Merek responded.

Feeling pressed for time, Merek hurried ahead and reached the last row of houses before North Street. Oil lamps shining through the second and third floors of windows in the merchant's houses helped the two young men climb up the side of one of the buildings.

Clambering past the second window, Pall froze in place when a man inside the house walked over to the oil lamp that was on a table in front of it. Merek, who was above him, had also stopped moving upwards.

Just then, a stronger gust of wind rattled the unglazed window and set it to shaking within its casement for a sustained moment. The man came closer to the window pane and tried looking out into the nighttime storm. Instead, he stared at the window, watching it, until the vibration stopped. When it stopped quivering, he shook as though with a sudden chill and turned away, picking up the oil lamp and walking outside the room with it.

Pall and Merek resumed climbing up the side of the building. Reaching the roof, they carefully and cautiously peered over the top of it to look at the view below them.

Pall saw that North Street, at almost thirty feet wide, was one of the widest streets in the city. It paralleled the northern defensive wall, which towered a bit over one hundred feet above the street. The city planners did not allow any buildings to exist within the shadow of the wall.

The two young men looked out at a two-hundred-foot expanse below them.

The full force of the storm pummeled them making them cling more tightly to the roof edge. Lightning rippled frequently across the sky.

Below them, on opposite ends of the open space, stood two armed groups facing one another. The southern group had the superiority in numbers, looking as though they had three to four times more men than the other side. Storm lanterns had been placed on the ground near the front and back ends of their line. Pall thought that this callous display of their position was an odd thing for these men to do. It puzzled and concerned him.

The northern contingent of men was bent in an arc towards their opponents. A man stood in the middle of it while another was in back standing on some kind of platform.

Merek and Pall watched as the giant of a man, for he towered over the backs of his men, strung his bow, nocked an arrow onto the bowstring and drew himself into the horns of his weapon.

211

There's something familiar about the way he moves, thought Pall.

Taking aim at the enemy before him, the archer released an arrow. A man who had been standing in the front line before one of the storm lanterns, dropped to the ground.

Pall again became mystified when the dead man's companions did not shout imprecations, or charge, against the men north of them. Instead, they applauded. Whether they clapped their hands in approbation for the skill of the archer, or for some arcane reason for the gallantry of the man who had just been killed, Pall remained mystified by it.

He saw that the archer had nocked another arrow onto his bowstring.

Pall leaned over close to Merek and said, "These men below us seem drugged."

Merek continued looking down upon the scene, finally commenting, "They could be, but I think they are filled with religious fervor. I am afraid that the way they have set the lanterns around them so indifferently means they are quite confident of their victory."

"Can you release some bolts into them from up here?"

"Yes, but you may have to steady me so I don't fall off this roof."

"Not a problem, Merek. Shoot as many as you like. We can move back and forth on the roof between every two releases. But, we are too exposed up here. Use five or six quarrels and then we need to get off this building and down onto the street."

Merek spanned the crossbow and set a bolt onto it. When he released the first one, the bowman had already begun firing his own arrows into his opponents.

When lightning went off again, Pall carefully watched the archer go into action. The young man smiled and laughed out loud.

"What's so funny, Pall?" Merek asked as he again spanned the crossbow's string.

"We both know the giant up ahead firing arrows into this lot below us," he said.

"We do?"

"Yes; that's John Savage. You stay up here. I think you can fire well enough without me. I've got to get down below. I'm useless up here."

Without waiting for a reply, Pall moved away from the peak of the roof, and climbed down the back side of the building. He saw light coming from the third floor. There was none coming from the floor below. Reaching the second story window where he had earlier seen the man trying to look out of it, he stopped at its base, positioning himself so that he could raise it open. It was dark inside the building and no light shone from any other inside source. The young man opened the window and entered the room.

The fury of the storm outside covered the sound of his footsteps inside the house. He found the hallway and then the stairs leading down to the first floor. Once on the first floor, he walked to the door, raised the bar across it and set it to the side.

Pall slowly opened the door and looked out at the backs of the men in the southern group. They had either doused their lanterns or shuttered them completely. He could see that some men were still falling from the combined shooting of Savage and Merek.

One of Savage's arrows was imbedded in the center of the door he had just opened.

The rain, impossibly, increased in its force. The wind stopped gusting and fell still. The thunder and lightning ceased. All that could be heard was rain pounding on everything beneath its incessant deluge.

The young man got a chill that he could not shake off of him. A darkness overwhelmed him. He wanted to sink to his knees. He heard a faint conversation occur that sounded as though it was happening in the middle of his head, but behind him as well. He felt as though spiders were crawling over his body.

Pall stood absolutely still. Waves of nausea rolled over him.

A whole chorus of wood thrush calls sounded.

The Üngers summoned by Kosem Mungadai in his scrying chamber had arrived to wreak their appetite and mortal destruction onto Savage and his men.

CHAPTER NINETEEN

Esender and Zhenjin were standing near one another in the front ranks when the giant archer started firing upon them and their men. Instead of being dismayed at his attack on them, they were elated, instead. Savage had revealed himself and done so in a major, ostentatious way.

When the first of their men fell prey to the street by the bowman's fatal aim, the two leaders led their men in a zealous and vigorous applause.

"Father Kosem Mungadai's spirit is favoring us," stated Zhenjin to his brother priest.

"Yes," Esender replied, "he has delivered our enemies into our hands right in front of us."

More of their men fell from the big man's accuracy with his longbow. One of Savage's arrows ricocheted off the street, whining by Esender's left hip. Miraculously, it did not hit anyone. The power behind the missile drove it deeply into one of the shop doors behind them.

Esender was keenly watching his men being hit by Savage's attack on them. "Something is not correct," he commented to Zhenjin. "Savage isn't the only one firing arrows upon us. Our men are falling from another archer shooting at them as well."

Just as the two priests started to look around to spot the second man, they felt the senses of darkness, enmity and hatred pour over them.

Zhenjin, elated from feeling the mélange of evil wafting through him, exclaimed excitedly, "Our Father has brought us the power we need to snuff out these fools who think they are going to destroy us."

"The three–in–one are here," said Esender with awe, referring to the Üngers. "There are many of them. They have brought others from the darkness with them."

Lightning flashed in the sky.

In the corner of his eyes, Zhenjin saw a small missile flash down from one of the roofs above and in back of their position. The next flash of lightning revealed a crossbowman on top of one of the buildings. The priest smiled with satisfaction.

"I have found the second man. He is releasing bolts from his crossbow above us on that roof there, which is in the center of our line here on the street. Let me speak with what is yet to appear in front of us. This man will soon have his doom sealed over him."

The air in front of the two priests began to roil and writhe with contorted, half formed shapes. The oppression of perversion and blight grew to an unbearable degree. Esender approached the area where the air had become alive with beings from another realm and stood within inches of it. As it became more distinct and shadows within the revolving air solidified, he began talking to it in an ancient tongue not known on this world except to the highest adepts of Mungadai.

Send three of the shaitans up that roof; bring the mortal to me that's up there urinating his quarrels down upon us. Destroy anyone who gets in your way.

One is enough, mortal priest, came a voice from the sinuously boiling air in front of him. *Do not waste our time with useless requests of our power. Or you will be micturating from that roof in lieu of the one you desire us to capture.*

Deeply chagrined by the invisible beings before him, both priests got down onto the wet street and paid due homage and obeisance to them.

Forgive us, O Great Ones, intoned Esender, *we but seek to destroy the blight and evil in the devils facing us.*

Careful for whom you call devils, O lesser than dust of this world. We will do what your priest sacrificed for—that and no more. Do not address us again, unless you are summoned to do so.

Esender and Zhenjin remained supine on the street. The cloud of malevolence was directly over them. Fifteen Üngers, including an equal number of jinns, imps and assorted demon like creatures

218

emerged from it. As they did so, they first stepped upon the shoulder blades of the two priests before they touched the street itself.

With their backs deeply singed from the impress of the spirits' feet stepping upon them, the two brother priests stood up on their feet with great difficulty. They were, however, ecstatic from being severely burned.

One jinn, a monster of a creature, took one bound off the street and landed on the roof where Merek was shooting down into Mungadai's men. He grabbed the crossbowman as though he were but a puling child.

The rest of the jinns, imps and demons went through the priests' men, getting into a rough formation on their right flank. As they moved between them, two jinns reached out and touched a man apiece. They became like burning torches. While they burned, they sang a holy song of a martyred death. The two remaining jinns picked their flaming bodies up without any apparent damage being done to them. They heaved them over the heads of Mungadai's followers towards the top of the arc of men facing them on the north side. Like Greek fire being thrown from two trebuchets, they traced a burning trajectory in the air. They landed on either side of Savage's platform and set it afire.

It was then that Esender and Zhenjin gave their men the order to charge.

The fifteen Üngers flashed into appearance. They spread out ahead of the southern force. Each one drooled burning spit from its mouth. The slaver fell to the street in sizzling loops of acidity and corrosiveness. When it hit the street, steam arose. The vapor immediately was blown down the east side of North Street.

Pall watched in growing consternation what was happening out on the street before him. He saw the roiling mass of air appear and the priests being humbled by whatever creature or evil deity spoke from it. He watched in stunned horror as a huge creature, obviously going after Merek, jumped up onto the roof above Pall. When the two jinns lit up two of what he had thought were Mordant's men, he was struck with the calloused disregard in which it was done. He was dumbstruck at the fanaticism of the men who, while burning, sang their song of victory.

The young soldier became incensed with anger and disgust when their burning bodies rained down on either side of Savage. While the priests' side charged Savage's position, Pall went with them, screaming at the men near him while they shrieked and roared at those upon which they were about to fall.

Savage, being aware that a crossbowman was on the roof exactly opposite from where he stood and shooting down onto Mungadai's men, started to laugh. They easily shot down fifteen or sixteen men between them. But something was wrong. The bowman could palpably feel it. His senses went into a hyperactive state of awareness.

When he saw the air rolling and writhing in front of two men who eventually started to pray to it, he knew why the men he had been shooting had acted so strangely by just remaining in place while they were being killed.

He watched with concern as a giant jinn leapt onto the roof of the building where the crossbowman was releasing a bolt into the men below him. The jinn pulled the man into his arms and jumped back down onto the street. He had tucked him under his right armpit and carried him into battle.

The archer fired more arrows.

He yelled at Red to pull their men back behind the platform from where he was shooting.

The men pulled back. Red came over to Savage and stood before him. "What in the name of the seven burning lakes in hell are those creatures?!" he shouted up to the bowman.

"They're exactly that. They've been summoned by powerful magic. We've got to fall back and run up onto the fortress wall. There's an access point right behind me."

One of Red's men ran up to him and pointed west onto North Street. "Red!" he shouted, "Look!"

Red and Savage turned to look.

Just then, two towering arcs of burning flame were flung high up in the air heading toward them from the direction of Mordant's men.

Savage yelled at those around him to start toward the north wall.

Reaching the highest point of their trajectory, the two burning missiles started their descent onto where Savage stood. When they landed on either side of the stand, Savage saw that they were human. He jumped away from the platform in disgust as it almost immediately started burning.

At the same time the bowman's feet landed on the ground, Mungadai's men charged against them.

Peredurus and Martains, having marched north on Farmers and Butchers streets, entered North Street where they reformed together at the intersection of Butchers and North streets. An incessant and driving rain aided by high winds had harassed them all the way from Center Street. After regrouping together, they sent three pairs of scouts east of them on North Street. They were to do a reconnaissance of what was ahead of them by no more than ten city blocks, and to reconnoiter back with the main force to report what they had found.

Within half an hour they returned and reported that Savage's force had been located seven blocks east of the Minister's current position. Savage's people were observed building what looked like a firing platform. They were just about finished with this task. Fifty to sixty of them were in place around the stand. Sentries had been posted fifty feet away from the stand on all but the north side. The main contingent had started to get in formation in front of the platform.

"Savage is getting ready for an attack on his position," said Martains.

"That likely means the priest's forces have gathered together and intend on overwhelming him. They outnumber him by three–and–a–half times," the Minister thought aloud to the Captain.

"They've got a bit over two hundred feet distance between the inner perimeter of the defensive wall and the other side of North Street where the last row of buildings there face it," replied the Captain.

"We don't have time to send half our men to the other side in order to squeeze them in the middle," offered Peredurus. "The street, despite its width, is too narrow for us all to go down at once. What do you suggest, Captain?"

"Place twenty–five men in three phalanxes apiece. Stagger them apart. Bring them up and halt them just out of sight of Savage. They go into his location in the following order: the first phalanx goes left, the second right and the third takes the middle. All three move forward at the same time and push the priest's men east away from Savage."

"What about the remaining eighty–six men, Captain Martains?" asked Braucus.

"Divide them in half, forty each, leaving six runners with us. Half are assigned to you and the other half to me. I'll go with the phalanxes. You take the other two groups and help out Savage. Assign Sergeants Meginhard and Burchard to each group of forty. Place a cordon of fighters around Savage and let him take it from there. If he is hurt or taken out, you'll have to command."

"Are you going to use all of the Aeonians in the phalanxes?

"No, we need them to leaven out our whole force, so we'll mix your men into the phalanxes and the elite fighters into the two groups," explained Martains.

"When do we engage Mungadai's forces?" asked the Minister.

"Send two of the runners as scouts forward. As soon as the battle begins, we'll move onto the street where they are fighting Savage. The scouts will come back and tell us it's time to move."

"All right, Captain. I think you've come up with an excellent strategy, especially given the circumstances and the conditions we're dealing with."

Quickly, as time grew more precious, Martains identified and organized seventy–five men who were to be placed into all three phalanxes. Both of the sergeants helped expedite this task. Those not picked for this assignment were divided into two groups. The Minister took charge of this effort.

When they were all in formation, two scouts were sent forward to observe the status of Savage's present position. They returned almost as soon as they were sent out, stating that the priest's men had already positioned themselves onto the south end of the prospective field of combat.

Martains put the three phalanxes into motion.

Peredurus, with the sergeants leading the two groups in back of the third phalanx, was between them.

The rain poured down without mercy. The wind blew as though guided by sheer ill will. The thunder boomed while lightning fanned out overhead in the sky.

The noise of their massed feet on the street resounded throughout the area. The sound bounced and echoed off the buildings and the northern defensive wall.

As they entered the street area where Savage and Mungadai's forces opposed one another, one of Red's men noticed their arrival.

Martains was shouting over the noise of the storm, getting the phalanxes aligned on the street the way he had described just moments before to Braucus and Peredurus.

Two burning objects were thrown into the sky towards Savage's position. Martains did not have time to study them carefully. His men were in motion, he could not stop them now even if he had wanted to halt them at that point.

The Captain saw the priest's men begin their charge to the north. Martains saw with satisfaction that his formation was about to smash into their western side and flank them.

Something powerful collided with the first phalanx and staggered the men in its front. Screams of men, swearing, fighting and dying assailed his senses.

He remained steady, focused on overseeing where the tide of combat would go; sounds and spectacle of battle were common to him.

The next set of bloodcurdling screams, however, was not so familiar to his combat experience. They were filled with absolute terror. He felt a sudden dread overwhelm him. He thought spiders were crawling all over his body. Voices, inarticulate, yet unseemly in their goatish glee, got into his head. He heard the sound of a human body being eviscerated. Then another. And another.

Several calls of a wood thrush went off next to the right side of his head.

Something powerful brushed by him and knocked him down onto the stone pavers of North Street.

The sounds of combat and men in mortal fear of what they were fighting against became louder than the storm beating down upon them. Lights appeared in most of the windows on the second and third stories of the buildings facing the northern wall. Windows went up without regard to the storm lashing against them.

The imps—attracted to the humans staring down onto the battle below, as well as to the warmth seeping out of the rooms—started scaling the walls to get to the windows in which such delicious food breathed down upon them.

One of the jinns became distracted by this alluring sight. It was carrying a crossbowman into the middle of the battle under one of its arms. The jinn watched the imps collectively push the priest's men into the far wall in order to get at the people in the upper quarters of the buildings. The imps were in a fury of desire to get at them. Several of them pushed the jinn out of the way, ripping away its grip on the man it was holding. The man's body fell down on the street.

The jinn snarled at them, picking one up and dashing its brains out on the street. Three more imps came to their fellow's aid. The fight that ensued between them killed three humans. Much mutual damage was also inflicted and shared between these demonic fighters. However, the end result was that they seemed to forget what they were fighting about when one of them pointed up at the edifices above them.

The other imps were assaulting the merchants and their families. Many had already entered the second and third floors. Some of them were throwing people out of windows to the imps below. Other people were being ripped apart in the rooms where they had been standing watching the battle occurring below them.

This melee to destroy humans above him, when it had just been on top of one of their roofs, was too much for the jinn to take. Ignoring the orders it had been given earlier by Mungadai, it eagerly joined the imps in their assault on the merchants and their families.

Bloodcurdling shrieks and demonic bellowing coming from these upper stories joined the sounds of the pitched battle on the street below.

Seventeen Slakes moved onto the scene from both sides of the combatants. They glowed from their recent conquests on Center Street. They were not selective on whom they attacked. If a Slake could be awed, these were in wonder over the number of men available to them. The Slakes were indiscriminate about whom they took.

As they erupted out of the streets to the south, they were closer to the priest's men. They took as many of them as their hunger allowed. As their hunger was bottomless, so was the amount of men they conquered.

Several Slakes, watching what the imps were doing, joined them in feeding on the humans in the buildings above them. The Slakes seemed to have no trouble in getting up the sides of the merchants' shops and homes. They seemed to float and glide effortlessly up along the walls in attacking them.

They did not have any scruples in taking men, women or children. They consumed anything that was human. Heaps and lumps of human sawdust began accumulating in the rooms from the Slakes' conquests. Some humans willingly let themselves be taken. It was immaterial whether or not they struggled against them, the result was the same in all instances. The wind, which had been yearning to get inside the open windows, now violently tore through them with released fury, scattering the mortal powder into chaotic patterns.

On the street itself, where the other Slakes had wreaked their havoc, piles of human dust appeared. They were quickly drenched by the rain and submerged in the runoff of water pouring away from the center of the road to nearby stone curbs on both sides of the street.

The Slakes, jinns, and demons, as well as the Üngers, started fighting one another over the human spoils they were accumulating so rapidly into their bodies.

Seven of the Üngers had split into their three parts.

A human massacre, an abomination of life and its natural order, as well as an internecine slaughter between the malevolent creatures, started to unfold.

Lightning went off over all of their heads, flickering like a hungry tongue trying to lick up the souls of those leaving their mangled and dead bodies.

CHAPTER TWENTY

Merek was in shock over what had just happened to him. Some kind of giant, nightmarish creature had jumped onto the roof where he had been releasing bolts from his crossbow into the men on the street closest to him. There was no time to be prepared for what occurred; it happened too quickly.

The thing easily carried him off the building onto the street below. It toted him into the midst of the battle where other, smaller demons knocked Merek out of the big monster's grip. He did not remember that he barely survived this encounter between these creatures. They were kicking, biting and gouging one another as he crawled away underneath them. Pieces of their bodies, along with the pouring rain, fell all around and on top of him.

He did remember that he was able to get up onto his knees. Between the hellacious bedlam of men and creatures in mortal combat with one another, he saw that he had been brought halfway to where Savage was in a desperate and losing fight with his men against Mordant's forces.

Merek crawled towards Savage. For some reason that he could not determine, he was unable to stand on his feet. He could feel the familiar sensation of an Ünger near him, but the perception was greatly

231

enhanced. It keened through him in a wail of pain and anger, and defeat, almost pinning him to the street.

There's more than one of them, he dully thought to himself as he wormed himself closer to the bowman.

His head pounded a steady rhythm of pain into his awareness. He could feel it deep down to the toes in his boots. He could not get up onto his feet. He had trouble catching his breath.

Come on, Joseph, stand up; you must stand up. The men need you; you need them.

"Captain Martains!" he heard a familiar voice exclaim over him.

He saw sparks fly as a sword fight occurred over his body. Something fell on him and then was kicked away.

"Captain Joseph Martains...."

He recognized this voice.

Another hand–to–hand fight ensued near his head. Blades striking against one other clanged sharply and shrieked as they were dragged along the metal length of each other. Sparks alighted over his eyes. He thought for a moment that he was alone at night looking deeply into the sky overhead. The constellations with which he was so familiar started collapsing, falling down onto the world like sparks from a shattered torch thrown from the ramparts of a castle.

A sword shattered in two on either side of him. He could feel the broken blade scream in its steeled anguish as it split apart.

"Martains, quickly now, lift up your right arm!"

The Captain found that his arm had done as asked, as if it had willpower independent of his own mind.

A powerful hand locked its grip onto the underside of his forearm.

His own hand grasped back.

He was on his feet and Sergeant Meginhard was moving him away from the annihilation being done to the men in the phalanxes.

The Captain could not comprehend what was happening until the Sergeant brought him near to Savage. He was placed in back of the burning platform the bowman had been shooting from at the beginning of the fight.

Light, with the incandescence of the sun, flashed on and off repeatedly in a hypnotic rhythm.

Captain Martains felt as though he was falling from a great height.

Red was torn into pieces in front of Savage by two jinns. They just reached out and grabbed Red from either side and pulled. Their harsh guttural laughter fell against the giant man next to them. The jinns ignored everything else going on around them at this point. They were in full battle lust. They started eating the pieces of Red's body, stuffing them into their mouths and swallowing the chunks whole.

Savage thought they stunk worse than pigs in their own offal on a blistering hot summer day. Their stink stung his eyes. He drew both of his anelaces from their sheaths that were belted on either side of his hips. Tears fell from him as he started slicing off their arms and gouging out their sides. The bowman was in an inhuman frenzy. His great height, strength, ferocity and desire for revenge overcame the jinns before they realized that a human being was overpowering them.

Disgusted with what he thought was the inadequacy of the anelaces he was employing on them, he sheathed them and picked up a double-edged longsword that had been dropped to the ground in another separate struggle. He grunted in satisfaction as he severed the head off of one of the jinns. The other jinn, being constrained by a missing leg and arm, tried to turn on the bothersome human with what looked like a needle.

Its head soon joined its companion's on the street at Savage's feet. Savage struck the sword point first in the second jinns' body and let it remain there. He bent down and picked up the two heads in both of his hands. He hurled them separately at targets that made themselves available to him. His first mark was another jinn whom he hit in the face as it was about to take a bite from a fresh human carcass it had just collected. The jinn caught the sundered head of his companion in his arms as it bounced off his own skull. It gave a snort of disbelief and started to gnaw on it.

Looking directly at Savage, as it chewed on the grisly prize it had in its hands, the jinn declaimed, *You will pay for this, mortal, for soon I will treat and eat you in the same way.*

Savage ignored the taunting demon, throwing the head of the second jinn he had killed at a monk from the Church of Equity. The force he used to hurl the jinns' head knocked out the man when it made contact with his temple.

Savage withdrew the sword out of the dead jinn and walked up to the third, pushing several men aside who were battling against one another. Around him were two Üngers, one of which had split into three. Four of them were sucking out the viscera of the victims they had caught. The jinn watched him approach with curious and beady red eyes.

Do you wish to take a chance and dance with me, puny one?

It stood up as tall as it could, threw the head it had in its hands at Savage and charged the big man.

Savage dodged the thrown head, which ended up hitting and breaking the ankle of one of his own men fighting nearby. The big man dodged again as the jinn went by him. The bowman was tall enough that he raised the longsword over his head with its point down. Just as the jinn went by him, he dropped the sword into the back of its neck, plunging it deeply into its body.

The jinn bellowed its anger and frustration at Savage, but the archer had no patience in being the subject of its threats. He moved deeper into the swarming field of combat. He saw and recognized Merek crawling toward him. He ran over to the young man, picked him up and carried him back to the now destroyed firing platform.

He was about to ask him if he had seen Pall, but an extraordinary commotion was occurring just west of him on the street. Savage looked out and saw that Peredurus, as well as a captain and two sergeants of the Aeonian Elite Guard had mustered the remaining force of their men together. They were formed up in the shape of a wedge. The phalanxes that the bowman had seen them in only minutes earlier had been destroyed. Every man who had been in them and survived was wounded in some way.

At great loss in manpower, they managed to get the wedge within twenty feet of where Savage stood with Merek. The wedge was smashed by a combination of Üngers, mortals, demons and remaining jinns.

The Slakes and imps were nowhere in sight.

He thought that Peredurus and his men were looking at him directly. When he shouted at them, they did not heed his call. The bowman turned around and looked in the direction towards which these men were staring. What he saw gave him the thrill of his fighting life.

Pall, in charging with what he thought were Mordant's men, ran unmolested by them. In the heat of the charge, the darkness amidst the flickering of lightning, the wind pushing against him and the rain gushing copiously out of the heavens, he failed to hear any of the noises and sounds of fighting. He thought, briefly, that his ears had failed him, or that they were blocked in some fashion that he did not understand.

He ran with Üngers next to him at times. Imps and a jinn, going in the opposite way, pushed him impatiently aside as they went back to the merchants' buildings on North Street. The defensive wall loomed ever taller over him as he approached the platform where he had first seen Savage releasing arrows into what he thought were remnants of Mordant's command.

Men running with him were singing, praying and roaring out their hatred for the unbelievers they were seeking to kill.

Others, victims of war on both sides, were provender for the insatiable desire that was lodged in the hearts of men and demons who sought alike to kill, to destroy, to maim them. These men cried, died and sighed out their last words in the midst of war's lust that so eagerly and greedily consumed them.

On the inside of the northern defensive wall, with no enemy to fight against on the other side, the remaining warriors trembled in the light of death and in the darkness of life, facing a terrible force unleashed against them within their own city walls.

One of the last of the women fighters on Savage's side was thrown to the street. Her jaw hit the pavement first as she was simply cast down by the frenetic power of a jinn hurling her to the ground with more than full force. Her teeth shattered in her mouth.

The rich, copper taste of blood filled her mind. Her life roared into her being and split apart from her. She died in an instant.

To his left, forty feet away, Pall saw one of the demon creatures carry Merek toward Savage's position. There was nothing he could do to help him. It was too far away and running at inhuman speed towards the northern wall.

The young man realized that he had no weapon in his hands. The quarterstaff was still slung over his shoulder. His falchion sword remained sheathed.

He was simply running like a sheep rushing along a penned-in runway towards the fleecing shed.

"No!" he shouted. "NO!"

He stopped running.

Other men bumped into him and swore at the young soldier. They pushed him out of their way.

Amidst the roaring of battle and the booming of thunder, he heard his father singing.

He felt his mother praying.

An adrenaline rush exploded within him and lifted him into an energy he had rarely ever experienced before except at the pinnacle of combat.

This is familiar to me. I have felt this before. I was born to wield this energy.

Pall, without realizing he had done so, had the two-headed quarterstaff in his hands. He was wielding it with the mastery his father had ingrained in him through constant hours of practice with a plain wooden one.

He watched himself swinging it, parrying blows, and knocking away hands, claws, weapons and even a woman who tried to climb on top of him while he was engaged in braining a man attacking him.

The young warrior worked his way towards where he last saw Savage.

Pall's efforts were attracting his enemies' attention. They started flocking to him and encircled him, waiting for a chance to knock him off his feet.

"Where are my companions when I need them?!" he roared.

Two jinns ran into him on both sides. One grabbed the quarterstaff away from him while the other picked him up and flung him into the air.

In midair, his instinct, practice and superb training and skill made him flip over. Before he landed feet first onto the street, his sword was in his right hand. As his feet hit the pavement, he sliced the arm off one of the jinns.

It yowled its hatred at the mortal who had the audacity to strike it. The jinn reached out with its other hand and discovered, even before the arm was fully extended, it was severed, too.

Pall espied Savage and cut a wide swath to his side through those attacking him.

Three Üngers, split into nine raging and drooling monsters, attacked the young warrior. They were useless against him. Pieces of them lay in the street, steaming from the rain hitting their mangled bodies. Men and demons ran away from him.

"Hello, John!" he said to Savage when he reached his side. "Been hoping you'd show up!"

The bowman laughed and said, "I see you know how to use that pointer you have in your hand."

The two men waded back into the fray of combat to get Merek. Pall fought ahead of Savage, thereby allowing the bowman to pick up Merek at the spot where the young man was still crawling to get to them. Pall, possessed with the frenzy of combat and guided by his maturity as a master fighter, created a space in which Savage was also able to bring Merek back to the ruined shooting platform.

Pall knelt down to check on Merek.

Savage guarded the two of them.

Pall took off his tattered cloak and put it over Merek.

"How are you doing, Merek?" he asked.

"Don't worry about me. I'm glad to see you. I thought I never would again. I tried, Pall," Merek said. He started coughing. Blood sputtered out of his mouth into his hand.

"You did fine, my friend. What you did on the roof was about as brave as brave is."

Another attack came at Savage, pushing him away from protecting the two young men in his charge.

Pall stood up and helped the bowman.

A jinn, and an Ünger in the form of a snake, joined the men attacking Savage and Pall.

It took too much time to dispatch them. In the corner of his eye, Pall watched helplessly as Merek went down to his death. The crossbowman was defenseless and easily overwhelmed by three fighters.

Esender and Zhenjin were ecstatic. They felt that they were at the culmination of greatness. A major victory was about to be clenched in their hands.

"Our Master has watched over and protected us!" Esender, who was looking as though he was going into a religious swoon, gushed.

"Indeed," responded Zhenjin in a similar rush of sentiment. "He has worked his will for our cause."

"We can start mopping up what's left of our vaunted opposition, who in vain were denied any victory."

The two men laughed, hugged one another. They started singing.

Their infectious joy spilled over to the other men still standing on their feet.

Soon, Kosem Mungadai's followers were singing a song of praise to him as they started the end of their combat operations.

CHAPTER TWENTY-ONE

The Minister was dumbfounded at the speed with which his confidence and men had been literally destroyed. He no longer saw the point of battling inhuman forces that seemed impossible to defeat. He started gathering his wounded together and, with the help of those not seriously injured, tried getting all of them to the nearest stairway at the base of the northern defensive wall.

They never made it to the stone steps. They were decimated before the entrance leading up to the ramparts above.

A large piece of broken pavement was prised from the surface of North Street. The imp doing it speedily removed it. Once in both hands, it threw the piece down on the stone surface nearby. The paver shattered into several sections. The imp cackled and giggled, arguing aloud to itself over what jagged fragment it was going to throw.

Its fellow combatants, impatient over the imp's antics, yelled at it in exasperation and anger because it was in the way of their own rush to kill Mungadai's enemies.

The imp, frustrated about what piece of stone it was trying to select, arbitrarily picked up the one nearest to its left hand. Once it was securely gripped, it stood up and ran toward the mortal with the pretty looking sword.

The creature could only get twenty feet from what it called *a breather*. There were too many of his companions trying to kill it. Beside the young one with the sword stood a giant of a man. The imp hissed and swore profusely. He realized he had two wonderful targets to hit. Yet, it only had one piece of paver to throw. It went through an additional cycle of cackling, giggling, cursing and arguing with itself.

Another imp came up to it and tried to take the stone away. The imp with the stone used it to brain its rival. As his opponent fell away, it grabbed the stone and dislodged it from the first imp's hand. The stone fell away to the ground and the imp, in sheer indignation over this fiasco, scrambled after it.

It felt around on the street with its hands and feet. Finally finding the piece of stone, its seething whimpering turned to a sort of ragged crooning. The imp picked it up. Its face broke out into a wild grin. The imp discovered with delight that the breathers battling in front of it were only fifteen feet away. With a shout of victory, the imp jumped high in the air and hurled the paver at Pall's head.

———————◄————►

Now behind the firing platform, Pall and Savage battled alone together. Martains temporarily remained where they had put him.

Pall watched in detached observation as a quarrel, released from a crossbow from someone in the crowd of opponents before them, penetrated deeply into the bowman's right upper thigh.

The young soldier felt himself becoming despondent, yet he continued fighting. He heard his father's voice telling him not to let his emotions rule the effect of his combat.

Anger, hurt, vanity, are all distractions, son. Keep your vigilance in force, let your sense of the sword and what it is for calm you.

Pall focused on merging himself into the rhythms of fighting in hand–to–hand combat.

He turned away from the archer to defend them from a vicious three–man attack. In the midst of battling them, he saw an imp jump in the air and hurl something at him. He did not react in time because his attention was absorbed by the three men trying to kill him.

The stone that the imp had thrown hit Pall in the back of his head. It struck him on the left side of his occipital bone.

Without meaning, or even wanting, to, the blow he sustained brought him to his knees.

245

Savage leapt into the place where Pall had stood and dispatched the three men quickly.

Sergeants Meginhard and Burchard, still able to fight with deadly skill despite their wounds, ran over to where Savage stood.

"Is the Sergeant all right, bowman?" Meginhard asked.

Savage looked more closely at his young friend and said to himself, *So, you are a sergeant in the elite Aeonian Guard.*

The bowman laughed in the satisfaction of knowing this fact.

Aloud, the big man asked, "Lad, are you going to be okay?"

Pall did not respond. His head was bowed. His eyes were closed.

The sergeants were now battling to protect Savage and Pall.

Five remaining Aeonian warriors made it over to the smoldering and destroyed shooting platform. They joined the two sergeants in defending the ruined stand, Merek's dead body, and Martains' crumpled form.

The lightning continued its eerie flickering.

The wind subsided.

The rain lessened, then jarringly and abruptly came to an end.

The change in the weather was so dramatic that all combat stopped. Men and demons alike looked up into the sky at the change.

The clouds that had loomed over them, since the sun had set on the previous day, raced by and were torn apart by a wind far above them that they could neither feel nor hear.

The moon could be seen. It shone in a refulgence of silver. Its light threw the water on the street into diamonds that sparkled and glittered everywhere one looked.

It is quiet, except for the shrill and raucous cries of crows.

The sun is shining.

Pall can feel its light shining on his legs.

He opens his eyes and cannot see anything. He feels like he is suffocating and realizes that there are bodies on top of him.

"It must be morning," he thinks.

He shrugs off two bodies that have fallen onto him. Standing up, he looks out at what is around him. To his shock and surprise, he is on a battlefield that looks very familiar to him. He realizes that he is near the Great Forest. The source of the Forgotten River is a short distance away from where he weakly stands.

The concussion on the back of his head is excruciating.

The dead lay all around him. They are in various positions of death where they had been struck down in their final moments of life. Their bodies are strewn in all directions until the end of his sight. Those still barely alive moan, curse and weep with deep lament and inconsolable grief.

Ravens and crows sing their own feeding songs of rapture on the corpses strewn so liberally and abundantly on the field of battle.

Pall wipes the gore of war off of him as best as he can with a fallen officer's cape.

He sees the sword his father made for him. He picks it up, wipes it clean and sheathes it into the scabbard at his side.

He does not bother to look for his knives. He knows they are irretrievably lost.

A wave of vertigo overpowers him. He closes his eyes and wipes his forehead with the back of his left hand.

He feels feverish to himself.

When he opens his eyes again, he finds himself wandering in the Great Forest he had first gone through with Savage in their approach to the farmstead. He remembers Savage calling it the Demesne of the Sentinels.

Oddly, time seems turned inside out and upside down to him. He watches Savage and himself run by where he stands next to a giant copper beech tree.

He looks more closely at the tree under which he stands.

He becomes disoriented when he discovers it is the Sentinel Tree under which he had battled the Ünger on the road to Gullswater.

How can this tree be present in the Forest as well as in the meadow where Tom and I placed his wagon? he asks aloud.

He hears a child laugh softly, and when he looks for the source of the sound of gentle laughter, he sees that other people are gathered under the tree with him, too: Alicia and Mary, the Herald, the giant Savaric, and his companions lost when he was a recruit in the battle against the Aeonian veterans.

He hears the silken rustling of a raven's wings moving in swift flight towards him. It flies by Pall, laughing darkly. One of its wings grazes his right arm as he wards it away from attacking him.

Laughing at him, the Valravn said, *What did I tell you, o man of mud, creature of clay, laborer of loess, about such a day as this….*

But Pall does not hear the rest of its bluster. His arm begins to burn with a fierceness that makes him gasp with pain. Sweat breaks out all over his body and soaks him thoroughly.

249

He becomes lost. Unhinged from life. Abandoned and left alone. There is no more anchor preventing him from drifting into oblivion because there is no meaning to life that he can fathom. He sees the world he has entered neither in black nor white. Everything is just bleak.

Someone touches him on his damaged arm. An even more exquisite pain courses through him from this contact.

Pall opens his eyes again and sees Herald standing before him.

The messenger is smiling gently at the young soldier.

Tears stream down Pall's face. Looking at Herald, all hope drains away from him. He feels empty. Light.

Guilt floods through him.

A woeful man am I.

Herald points into the field before the tree where Pall observes two people approaching him where he stands underneath its canopy.

The young man cannot determine who is there. He falls to his knees from vertigo and fever from the Valravn's attack on him.

Herald touches him on his head where he has received such a grievous wound.

Pall's dizziness and weakness pass by. He looks more attentively at the two people coming toward him.

One is a man in a white shimmering robe.

The other is Evangel.

Evangel! he cries.

She smiles with the appearance of an angel.

He knows that his love for her is forever.

It is immortal.

Instead of responding to him, she looks at the man by her side.

The man approaches Pall and helps lift him to his feet. His touch is firm, replete with a power that is filled with hope and wonder and deep joy.

Pilgrim, he hears the man call him, *darkness is upon the surface of this world wherein you live. It is time for the children of God to be revealed. You must awake and arise into the fullness of your maturity and power. The God of Armies is besides you. The Lord's Spirit is upon you. I am with you.*

The young soldier gasped and breathed air into his lungs as though he had not done so for an eternity.

He became aware that he was being held in Captain Martains' arms.

Sergeant Meginhard and Sergeant Burchard, alongside five Aeonian Guards, stood in place around them. They had formed a protective fighting ring encircling the Captain, Savage and Pall.

251

Mordant's men, staying in place, faced them.

The remaining demons released by Mungadai were filled with an avid and dread ache to finish consuming the priest's enemies.

Savage, limping from a horrid looking wound in his thigh, was in front of him. He was improvising and singing an off–key song in oppositional counterpoint to Esender and Zhenjin's men, who were chanting their own dire song of destruction.

Except for the singing, everything else was quiet. No one was fighting. They were all staring up at the moon overhead.

The Captain, seeing that Pall had recovered, beseeched him, "What are you waiting for, Sergeant Warren? Call upon the Risen Lord as you did that day when you saved me; let's drain this foul tide away from us!"

In the midst of the battle that was precipitated to a halt over sheer wonder in the dramatic change in the weather, Pall stood with Captain Martains' help. The young sergeant spoke aloud. Everyone in the street who was still alive, and could hear him, listened intently to his words. Blood dripped down onto his neck and shoulders from the wound on his head.

Sergeant Burchard ripped a shirt off one of the Aeonian dead. He handed it to Pall who cleaned the residue of battle still remaining on the falchion's blade off it.

He carefully sheathed his sword.

Looking up at the moon hanging above them in its full glory and splendor, he half sung and chanted,

"I am but a helpless fool, lost in the weight of this world's burden.

Around me has been a storm of hunger, guilt and grief, a curtain

of isolation that has but cast a pall of misery around this life.

I have solely tried to overcome evil and, yet, in the war and strife

against it, I have only been able to see loss and pain and death.

Judge through me this filth, now, I ask humbly with my last breath."

A jinn started to laugh in a deep guttural chuckle.

Pall turned to it and held up his right hand, palm first, toward the fiend. In a faint adumbration, a wave of heat poured out. It looked like vapor rising from a boiling pan of water brought outside into the chill of winter.

Esender and Zhenjin were standing less than ten feet away from Pall. They both screamed orders for the young warrior to be run through the heart.

The jinn that was laughing roared out a challenge to this puny looking little man and started running at him.

A white light coruscated out of the palm of Pall's hand. It flickered like the lightning had done earlier, and then steadied into a solid stream of light.

He turned the light erupting from his hand onto the jinn itself. It cut through the creature like it was thin paper. The jinn exploded apart.

He raised his other hand toward the moon. A beam of light flickered out of his palm and steadied into another solid beam of light.

The bowman closed his eyes.

"Pall," Savage urged, "bring the two together over our heads."

"So be it said," replied Sergeant Warren.

The young man struggled in complying with the bowman's direction, as though the light beams were incredibly heavy and difficult to move. He finally was able to put up both palms in the air and successfully crossed the beams against one another.

A large whining sound started to occur when the beams made contact together. Sparks started to drop to the ground.

The two priests charged Pall with their long knives bared.

A circle of light erupted out of the center of the light beams and fell away from them. It expanded to the full perimeter of the area where the battle had been fought.

Like a meteor falling out of the heavens, it fell on everything and everyone around them. When it exploded, no sound was emitted.

The searing white light that came next burned the retinas of anyone and anything watching it. The light turned black, green, violet, purple and blue.

So be it finished, Savage thought.

The bowman took his arms away from his eyes and opened them.

EPILOGUE

In Kosem Mungadai's soothscrying room, images begin swirling on one of the walls. Shapes shift back and forth from one another, transforming themselves into a variety of abstract patterns. Lights sweep rapidly from mirror to mirror and throughout the room faster than the human eye can follow. Words appear in midair and within the mirrors. Voices are heard, fade out, and then come back again into hearing, if anyone had been in the room and cared to listen to them. Of the many tongues being uttered, English, French, Mandarin, Arabic, Hopi, Aramaic, Sanskrit, Greek and Russian languages can be discerned.

Their voices caress the black marbled font upon which the irradiated image of the priest's shadowed remains is outlined now in red on its surface. He has become a frozen revenant of evil. Water from the font spills over his impression in the face of the dark stone; it is as though the ichor of darkness weeps over him. Soon, the room becomes silent. The water stills. The light in the room becomes murky, deadly somber and atramentous.

Something flickers, or jumps, as though an old movie reel slips out of its sprockets and disturbs the viewer's sense of reality. Seconds, minutes, hours pass by in rapid succession and at a rate far surpassing the normal speed of diurnal and nocturnal time. Being dark within the room adds to the impression that one is passing through vast expanses of space—it unfolds and flows in sidereal splendor.

A faint light brings the room into a murky focus. Within the mirrors, men and other beings are seen dimly. They are in a type of speakeasy viewing a visual transmission upon which their gazes are transfixed with greed. Their avarice is sharpened by the fact that what they are doing is illegal. If caught in their illegitimate delectation, they could be given life, even death, sentences by the reigning coalitional government.

A sign on the wall blinks out a four word phrase:

"Garden of the Hesperides"

If looked at too long, an after image in violet forms. It resides now between the eyes of the viewer, as though the optic nerves are permanently irradiated with its imprinted gestalt.

Gathered in a circle, these viewers are watching a five–dimensional hologram of Savage. Numbers and abstract symbols scroll underneath his image as well as above him. The bowman's mental and physical functions, along with his weapons, combat skills, reaction time and intelligence are also displayed in real time on a set of colored graphs, which can be affixed into space anywhere the audience's thoughts wish to peruse them. They are betting illegally on a variety of outcomes based on parameters computed by a sentient computer affixed within a table set in the middle of them. Smoke swirls through their encircled conclave, turning the scene into an opaque white haze.

Once more, the light in Mungadai's chamber snuffs out.

Another scene comes into sharp, brilliant focus. Vast plains, and rugged mountains corrugated between, them sweep by the mirrors. A rural landscape in what used to be the Utah high plains is portrayed in them.

The ground below is passing rapidly underneath a vehicle, which is intelligent. Through the western side of its transparent skin can be seen the late afternoon sun, whose outline is being oddly magnified and refracted by a scrim of thin, high flung clouds. The clouds help leach the color of the sun into a strangely filtered light that gives it a febrile, yet stunningly lit, cast.

Despite being the height of summer, the sun looks as though it is set in a midwinter sky and a blizzard is about to descend onto the surrounding land. Some of the suffused rays emerging from its orbed surface pulse faintly, burning silently above them in a subdued violet to purple violence.

A woman's voice remarks, "Look, they must have begun the test. Do you see it?"

"Yes," a male voice responds, "they have placed a pall between the star and the earth."

"Are we in danger of any radiation?" she asks worriedly.

"The danger is not in the clouds themselves, dear, but what they portend," he answers her.

"Is there hope for us mere mortals?" she asks now with dread because she sees he is fearful, too, of the sky above them.

"There is always hope, but not if we remain lost in the vanity and false pride of our technologies."

"So, there is little hope left then," she said in a faint voice.

"Yes, there is but a scant remnant remaining."

"Where can it be found now?" she queried one last time.

"In the heart of a penitent spirit in a human being," he said softly.

259

He mentally positions the vehicle to operate on its own cognizance in the tunnel. Just before it becomes stygian black, he reaches out to her and holds her left hand with his own shaking one.

End of *THE PENITENT– PART III*

Post a Review

If you liked reading *THE PENITENT – PART III,*
please post a review at immortalitywars@gmail.com.

CAST OF CHARACTERS

Moro Asutuo (also known as "**the dark one**"): Commander **Gregor Mordant's** chief of intelligence. The dark one lives on the Forgotten River in Gullswater. Many residents of the town think he is a simple recluse. His place has become the center of Mordant's northeastern intelligence network. The information Asutuo gathers together is eerily reliable. He is an indispensable worker for the commander. Asutuo works closely with the thaumaturge **Kosem Mungadai**.

Ailwin Athdar: The Abbot of **Dawn's Abbey**, a cenobium, or monastery, for men located in the Vale of Naomhin in the Western Isles.

Sergeant Burchard: A veteran soldier of the elite **Aeonian Guard**, serving in the Northern Army of **Ranulf Ealhhere**, King of West Fündländ.

Cébhfhionn (also known as "**Fair Locks**"): The name of **Bard Diarmad Somairhle's** harp. This harp is considered one of the chief instruments of the **Risen One**.

Sir Trevelan du Coeur: The High King's Champion of the Realm of the Western Isles. He becomes the

262

protector and sponsor of **Evangel Blessingvale** and her adopted grandfather, **Matthew Greatworth**.

Tom & Alicia Cooper: A married couple who are the parents of fraternal twins, **Mary** & **Myra Cooper**. Tom has been hired by the Town of Gullswater to be its new cooper.

Demesne of the Copper Beeches (also known as the "**Demesne of the Sentinels**"): These trees stand as **Sentinels** of the northern forest. A few humans know them as **the Wood of the Royal Guard**. They are sentient, puissant and mighty beings protecting this part of the world.

Ranulf Ealhhere: King of West Fündländ.

King Warin Ealhhere: Ranulf's father.

Altan Esender: One of **Kosem Mungadai's** assistants. The thaumaturge appointed Esender to head his southern fighting force in Seascale. His name translates roughly as "one who is goldenly alive with true health", or, "a true giver of gold and good health".

Captain Eumero: Captain of the longboat *La Signora Maria* (*The Lady Mary*). Eumero was in charge of seagoing operations for **Mordant's** northeastern intelligence network.

Giles: A follower of **Kosem Mungadai**, as well as a spy working for **Commander Gregor Mordant**.

Evangel Greatworth (also known as "**the Lady from the Wood**" or "**the Lady of the Fields and Forest**"): Her adopted grandfather, **Matthew Greatworth**, gave her this name; after finding her placed in a ditch for safety by her mother from outlaws. Both her parents and the members of their caravan were brutally murdered. Her given name is **Jacquelyn Blessingvale**.

Her first name, Evangel, means "Good News". Throughout the Western Isles, her birth name has been combined interchangeably with her given and last names.

Evangel Blessingvale, under the sponsorship of Sir Trevelan du Coeur and the auspices of the High King and Queen of the Western Isles Realm, united the military forces to defend its sovereignty, which is under domestic and foreign attack.

Her charismatic qualities, spiritual depth and direct connection with **the Risen One** have made her a driving force of reform in the Western Isles.

Herald: A messenger of **the Risen One**.

Lawrence: A young boy who waits tables and works at the Gullswater Tavern in Gullswater, West Fündländ.

Lucas: The owner of the livery stable in Gullswater, West Fündländ. He is married to **Mrs. Lucas**. One of their children is a son named **Lucas Junior**.

Captain Joseph Martains: A captain of the elite Aeonian Guard who serves as an adjutant to **High Marshall Solace Umbré**. Both men serve in the Northern Army of **Ranulf Ealhhere**, King of West Fündländ.

Marta Matasan: Prioress of St. Åyrwyus Priory, a priory for women located on the River Wythe in the Vale of Naomhin in the Western Isles.

Sergeant Meginhard: A veteran soldier of the elite **Aeonian Guard**, serving in the Northern Army of **Ranulf Ealhhere**, King of West Fündländ.

Merek (also known as "**Second**" or "**Twin**"): A member of Commander Gregor Mordant's Marauders. He and **Carac** are identical twins. He is extremely proficient with the crossbow.

Commander Gregor Mordant: The leader of **Mordant's** Marauders, he officially serves as a key member of King Ranulf Ealhhere's intelligence service. However, Mordant's loyalty is to the priest **Kosem**

Mungadai, head of the **Church of Equity** in Seascale, West Fündländ.

Kosem Mungadai (also known as **"the priest"** or **"father of us all"**): a thaumaturge of the 13th level in the occult arts. His origins are unknown. He is capable of great feats of organization and oratory. He communicates with what he terms "the darknesses" and divines what needs to be done in this world to satisfy their demands upon him. The priest has attained and been given the power to create magic, spells, and demonic creatures, as well as summoning these darknesses into his scrying chamber set within a secure room in his monastery.

He is considered a savior by his followers. He is well respected in the port city of Seascale where he has his monastery called the **Church of Equity**. However, Mungadai is a nihilistic spokesman, prophet and leader of a terrorist organization seeking to destroy all norms of government, including religious, monetary, military and economic societal orders.

Mustard (also known as **"Gordo"** or **Gordon**): A member of **Commander Gregor Mordant's** Marauders.

Nigel: A spy working for **Commander Gregor Mordant**. He is also a close associate of **Kosem Mungadai**.

Braucus Peredurus: King Ranulf Ealhhere's Minister of Affairs, Foreign & Domestic. The minister was appointed by the King to be in charge of all governmental concerns, foreign and domestic. Peredurus has held this position for many years, bringing a wealth of experience in political strategy and knowledge about the conduct of war and peace to the crown.

Braucus, at the age of nine, started an apprenticeship of study with his father that lasted until his father's death, when Braucus was thirty–one.

Lycidyuse Peredurus: Braucus' father who served under **King Warin Ealhhere**, who, in turn, was the father of the present king, Ranulf Ealhhere. Lycidyuse was the former Head of the Admiralty for **King Warin Ealhhere's** maritime and naval forces.

The Risen One: A reference to the spiritual reality known on **old Earth** as **the Messiah**, **Yeshuah Hamashiach**, or **Jesus the Christ**. His name, personage and divinity have been banned by the major religious orders in the Western Isles, West Fündländ and other contemporary realms. Severe to capital punishment is meted out to those who mention His name and/or worship Him and follow His teachings.

High King Peter Áed Menn Rochtmar: The High King of the Western Isles.

High Queen Isolde Bébhinn Menn Rochtmar: The High Queen of the Western Isles.

John Savage (also known as **"the bowman"** or **"the archer"**)**:** Plays a major leadership role in **King Ranulf Ealhhere's** intelligence. Savage works directly under the command of **Braucus Peredurus**, the King's Minister of Affairs.

Savaric (also known as **"the giant"**)**:** A veteran soldier of the elite **Aeonian Guard**, serving in the Northern Army of **Ranulf Ealhhere**, King of West Fündländ.

Diarmad Somairhle: One of the Western Isles greatest bards in its history. He was given the formal title of **"the Ri–Eigeas, the Priméces, the Bard of the Realm of the Western Isles, Filidhe Diarmad Somairhle"**. His mastery of his craft is legendary. The musical, psychological and spiritual connections he has with his harp, **Cébhfhionn**, is recondite, mystical and transcends normal human abilities and understandings.

Although relatively unknown, bard and harp have a longstanding relationship with **the Risen One**.

Stephan & Glenda Sayer: Sayer is head of the Great Bay Merchants Guild. He is also one of the chief proprietors of the Great Bay Tavern. He works undercover for **Braucus Peredurus**, especially in communications. There are some who question his loyalty to the Minister of Affairs, but nothing definitive can be claimed against him in this regard.

    Glenda is his wife, who also plays a role in intelligence gathering and spying along with her husband.

Slake: Created into being in the world by **Kosem Mungadai**, a Slake is a stunningly beautiful woman creature whose skin color is multihued. Slakes have irresistible sensual and sexual appeal to humans regardless of the fact that they are prey to the monsters' unquenchable craving for consuming them.

    When the Slake is done feeding on a human being, the body of its victim turns to dust. The self that belonged to the human is used by the Slake to keep its form in the corporeal world. If the Slake cannot obtain another victim, it has to return to the darkness from which it originated, taking the consciousness of its victim with it.

Professor Melvin Tobin, Ph.D. (2065–2189): A former internationally known and respected professor. Upon retiring, he was unanimously granted the status of emeritus professor by his peers at **Harvard University** in Cambridge, Massachusetts on Old Earth. During his research and teaching years at Harvard, Professor Tobin held three endowed chairs in Philosophical Systems, Intelligence Engineering, and Quantum Genetics. He was a specialist in evolutionary intervention.

Ünger: A name of a class of demons, individually and collectively, created by the priest **Kosem Mungadai**, leader of the **Church of Equity**. It has the capacity to divide itself into three separate creatures in the respective shapes of a snake, a lizard and a panther.

The Ünger is completely inimical to human beings. It can be difficult to see because of its peculiar qualities in moving from place to place, as well as its shape shifting features in going from transparent, blurred to opaque states of being.

It is almost impossible to kill. It destroys human beings by eviscerating and consuming all of the internal parts of the body, leaving the external skin and hair intact.

High Marshall Solace Umbré: The leader of the elite **Aeonian Guard**, serving in the Northern Army of **Ranulf Ealhhere**, King of West Fündländ.

Valravn: John Savage best describes this powerful entity. "A Valravn is a supernatural bird. Its name means raven of the slain. Eating the heart of a king on a field of battle as it told us, means that it's become a terrible animal."

David & Lucia Warren: Pall Warren's biological father and stepmother. Formerly the High Commander of **King Ranulf Ealhhere's** Northern Armies, he retired early to become a master blacksmith in a small village in West Fündländ.

Pall Warren: Raised in a small village in West Fündländ by **David** and **Lucia Warren**, Pall becomes one of the finest young warriors of his time. He is especially gifted in hand–to–hand combat with the quarterstaff, falchion sword and fighting knives. He has been deeply touched by the **Hand of God**.

Abagha Zhenjin: One of **Kosem Mungadai's** assistants. The thaumaturge appointed Zhenjin to head his northern fighting force in Seascale. His name translates roughly as "an uncle of true gold".

News about the Rest of the Series

With the end of the first trilogy completed, the next two are being planned. Please stay in touch with Keith's progress in writing *The Immortality Wars* series at:

https://immortalitywars.com/

ABOUT THE AUTHOR

A. Keith Carreiro earned his master's and doctoral degrees from Harvard Graduate School of Education, with the sequential help and guidance of three advisors, Dr. Vernon A. Howard, Dr. Donald W. Oliver and Professor Emeritus, Dr. Israel Scheffler. Keith's academic focus, including his ongoing research agenda, centers upon philosophically examining how creativity and critical thinking are acquired, learned, utilized and practiced in the performing arts. He has taken his findings and applied them to the professional development of educational practitioners and other creative artists.

Earlier in his teaching career he was a professor of educational foundations, teaching graduate students of education at universities in Vermont, Florida, Arizona, and Pennsylvania. He currently teaches as an adjunct professor of English at Bridgewater State University, as well as teaching English, philosophy, humanities and public speaking courses at Bristol Community College.

His research on creativity and critical thinking is based upon his experience in learning and performing on the classical guitar. He started studying this instrument at the age of four with Maestro Joseph Raposo, Sr., and took lessons with him until the age of 17. Keith also studied music theory and composition with Maestro José da Costa of New Bedford, and classical guitar with Robert Paul "Bob" Sullivan of the New England Conservatory of Music.

In 1973 at Ithaca College, he attended a master class workshop conducted by Miguel Ablóniz of Milan, Italy. Ablóniz' knowledge about technique and aesthetics attained a worldwide influence about the nature of guitar practice and performance. Maestro Andrés Segovia considered Ablóniz to be one of the world's most esteemed classical guitar teachers.

During the 70s, Keith performed his music and selections from the classical guitar repertoire throughout North and South America. He had many opportunities to play with a wide variety of musicians, composers, singer/songwriters, choreographers, theater directors, performers and conductors.

Due to his love of family, he has seen his fervor for history, as well as his passion for wondering about the future, deepen dramatically.

He lives in Swansea, Massachusetts and has six children and 13 grandchildren. He belongs to an eighty-five-pound golden retriever and an impish Calico cat.